A Spoonful of Sugar

A Spoonful of Sugar

A Bachelor Bake-Off Romance

Kate Hardy

TULE
PUBLISHING

Chapter One

January

TYLER FROWNED AND sniffed the air. Was that burning he could smell?

Oh, no. He made a dash for the kitchen, to discover smoke coming out of the stove. Three seconds later, the smoke alarm started shrieking.

"Way to go, Carter. How to make the neighbors happy—not," he said with a groan. He turned the stove off, then grabbed a dish towel so he could pull the cake out of the stove. The problem was obvious right away: the cake batter had spilled over the sides of the cake pan and the bits that had fallen onto the floor of the stove had burned. Great. So now he was going to have to clear that up, too, once the stove had cooled down.

He dumped the cake pan on the stove top, then frantically flapped the dish towel underneath the smoke alarm in the hope that the air would stop it.

Nope: it was still shrieking.

What was he going to have to do to shut it up? Take out

the battery?

And if one of his neighbors called the fire brigade… Just no. He'd never live it down. Quite a few of the firefighters trained in Carter's Gym—which was next to the Wolf Den dive bar in Marietta, opposite the fire station—and Tyler had a pretty good idea of the sort of jokes he'd have to put up with for the next six months if any of the fire crew found out about this.

It had been bad enough last time, when he'd made grilled cheese for his lunch at the gym and forgot about it for just long enough to set off the smoke alarm. The fire crew had teased him for months.

Why, why, *why* had his team entered him into this Bachelor Bake-Off thing? It was a crazy idea. He was just about the worst person they could've entered.

The smoke alarm continued shrieking. He opened the kitchen window, hoping that a blast of cold fresh air might make a difference.

It didn't.

And then the doorbell rang.

Half of him was tempted to ignore it. Then again, if it *was* one of his neighbors, he'd better explain that things were almost under control and he wasn't actually burning down the apartment block.

When he opened the front door, he was surprised to see Stacey Allman standing there. She'd moved into the apartment next door to him about six months ago and he didn't know his neighbor that well—enough to say hi to her in the lobby and to take in the occasional parcel for her. But she'd always seemed very sweet, albeit shy. Pretty, too, with her dark-blonde hair cut in a tousled style, a heart-shaped face and blue-grey eyes.

Not that Tyler was looking to get involved with anyone. He was still getting his head together over what had happened with Janine. Right now he was happy to concentrate on building up his business and forget all about love.

"Are you OK?" Stacey asked.

"Uh, I just set the smoke alarm off," he said. Talk about stating the obvious. She could hear that well enough for herself. "Sorry I disturbed you." He'd better apologize to his other neighbors this afternoon, too.

"It's not a problem—I'm not here to complain. I was just b-b—" She took a deep breath. "Being neighborly, in case something was wrong." She looked at him, and the desperation must've been written all over his face because she asked, "Do you need some help?"

Did he need help? A miracle, more like. Tyler didn't have a clue what he was doing and he really didn't want to make a complete idiot of himself in front of the whole town.

Then he remembered that sometimes he'd walked past Stacey's door and smelled something gorgeous cooking— sugar and vanilla, so he'd just bet it had been cookies or cupcakes. Plus he knew she was a teacher, so she would be the ideal person to help him through the next few weeks. But

ne time he didn't want to be a nuisance. It wasn't
pect a near-stranger to drop everything for him.

igh she *had* been the one to make the offer…

aked a hand through his hair. "Yes, I probably do
he help," he admitted. "You know the Bake-Off that
mber of Commerce is holding to raise money for
House? Well, it turns out that all my staff at the gym
e of the clients clubbed together to pay for my entry
hundred dollars." He grimaced. "I had a word with
cCullough, who's organizing it, and I offered to
ive times what my team paid to sponsor my entry if
t me off the hook. But she said no. I have this nasty
they're all enjoying the idea of making me do baking

cause, as a gym owner, you always eat healthily and
ver eat cake?" Stacey asked.

o, because I'm the world's worst cook and they know
ut all the time." He groaned. "The first round of the
Off is in two weeks' time and I'm going to make such
ot of myself. I just tried to make a layer cake as a
te because this Internet site said it was the easiest cake
ind I swear I only turned my back on the stove for
seconds to check my email…"

ie laughed. "And that's when the smoke alarm started
off?"

le gave her a rueful smile. "Yup."

Layer cakes can be tricky," she said.

4

He shook his head. "Now I know you're just being nice. I was a total failure, and I'm happy to admit it. I just need to work out what I did wrong."

"I do quite a b-bit of baking. Maybe I could help you," she offered, her cheeks turning pink.

That would be perfect. But he really didn't know her that well and it wasn't fair to expect her to pick up the slack for the stuff he'd never bothered learning to do. "I couldn't impose on you like that."

"I don't mind. Really."

She gave him another of those sweet shy smiles, and Tyler had to rein himself in mentally. She was his neighbor. He was *not* supposed to start thinking of her in a mushy way when she smiled at him.

"What do you need?" she asked.

"Why don't I make us some coffee?" he offered. "Come in—if you can stand the smell of burned cake and the noise of the smoke alarm—and I'll tell you about the Bake-Off."

TYLER'S KITCHEN WAS a complete mess. There was flour over most of the work surfaces and it looked as if he'd used every bowl and spoon he owned. There was a pile of dirty crockery next to the sink, and then on the stove top was a shallow cake pan. There was burned batter on the outside of the pan, and the center of the cake had sunk. Stacey could see exactly what had gone wrong.

Tyler was right: without help, he was going to come last in the Bake-Off fundraiser. With a very big gap between him and the next person.

But the first thing they needed to deal with was the smoke alarm. "Do you have a dish towel?" she asked.

"I've already tried flapping it under the smoke alarm," he said. "As you can hear, it didn't work."

"Damp or dry?" she asked.

"There's a difference?" Looking totally stunned, he handed her a dish towel.

"May I?" She gestured to the sink.

"Go right ahead."

A few seconds later, she'd splashed the dish towel with water, squeezed it out, and flapped the now-damp dish towel under the smoke alarm.

Finally, it stopped shrieking. And the silence felt almost defeating.

"Thank you. And I think I can say thank you on behalf of the rest of the neighbors in our block," Tyler said ruefully. "You've just more than earned that coffee."

"No problem," she said. "I once had a roommate who always set the fire alarm off whenever she cooked. That's how come I learned that damp dish towels work faster than dry ones."

"I'll remember that."

Tyler might not be any good at baking, but Stacey noticed that he did have a really fancy coffee machine. Even if it did have a slight covering of flour right now.

"How do you like your coffee?" he asked. "I can do latte, cappuccino, flat white…"

"A cappuccino would be lovely, thanks. With a spoonful of sugar, please," she added.

"One cappuccino with a spoonful of sugar coming right up," he said, and swiftly made two coffees. She noticed that he took his without milk or sugar, and it made her feel slightly guilty for taking the less healthy option. But she'd always taken her coffee sweet and milky.

She also noticed how beautiful his hands were. Well, the whole of Tyler Carter was beautiful, from his short dark hair to his sea-green eyes to his ready smile. His long-sleeved T-shirt was close-fitting and, given that he owned a gym and ran quite a few of the classes himself, Stacey was pretty sure he'd have a washboard stomach to go with the perfect musculature of his arms. And she wasn't even going to think about how toned his butt looked in his faded jeans.

He was way, way out of her league and she'd better not get any stupid ideas. She could hear her father's voice echoing in her head. *You're so dumb, Stacey…*

She pushed the thought away. Not here, not now. Tyler was her neighbor and she was doing the neighborly thing. "So tell me about Harry's House," she said when he ushered her through to his living room. "I don't really know anything about it."

"The local chapter of the Montana First Responders is doing up a house on the corner of 2nd and Church Avenue—it was left to the city and it's been vacant for years. The Chamber want to convert it to a Boys' and Girls' Clubhouse—the kind of place where kids can hang out after school and at weekends, get help with their homework, and use as a safe place," he explained. "The city said yes as long as we can bring the house up to code within ninety days. If they can't do that, then another development group is going to step in and buy the house. The First Responder chapter here in Marietta said they'd help out with the work and repairs, and they want to spearhead the fundraising and name the house in memory of Harry Monroe."

"Harry Monroe." The name was vaguely familiar. "Is he related to the Monroes at the grocery store on Main?" she asked.

"Yes; he was their son. He was a firefighter and an EMT—he used to come and train in my gym, and he was one of the nicest guys I knew," Tyler said. "He'd been visiting his fiancée in Bozeman on Labor Day. On his way back to Marietta, he stopped to change a flat tire for an elderly couple—just the sort of thing a guy like Harry would do—and he was killed by a hit-and-run driver."

Stacey put her hand to her mouth in horror. "Oh, no, how awful! His poor family. I hope whoever did it was caught?"

"Nobody was ever caught," Tyler said grimly. "The elderly couple didn't get a license plate and they couldn't even give a good description of the car—maybe they were too shocked to take it in, and it happened so fast. Though at least they had a cell phone with them and managed to call for an ambulance. But Harry had severe internal injuries and died at the hospital here in Marietta before they could get him to the operating room."

"The poor man. That's terrible."

"So that's why the fundraising's happening," Tyler said. "As I said, there's an investment company looking into buying the house and the First Responders don't want it bought out from under them. The local chapter is helping with the work, and so are other local businesses—even some of the vocational education students from the high school and community college are helping. Someone came up with the idea of a Bachelor Bake-Off to raise money, challenged local businesses to send someone along to compete."

He gave her a rueful smile. "I knew about the fundraising and I'd planned to donate money and prizes, but my team just couldn't resist nominating me. They'd signed me up before I had any idea what they were up to. And it seems that a few of our clients chipped in with the sponsor money, so I can't make up any excuses—I'd be letting too many people down."

"So what do you have to do on the Bake-Off?" she asked.

"What feels like the impossible," he said with a sigh. "There are three rounds held over the space of two weeks, and apparently I have to bake cookies, a pie and a cake." He ticked the items off on his fingers. "Except it all happens in front of people—we can't just bake stuff at home and rock up with it." He spread his hands. "Well, at least I'm making a prize idiot of myself in public for a really good cause. Maybe I can slap a dollar fine on everyone I catch laughing at me at work, to add to the funds."

"You really don't cook?" She'd never met anyone before who didn't cook at all, even if it was only grilled cheese or a simple omelet.

"I really don't cook," he said. "There are enough good places to eat in Marietta that I don't need to."

"So I guess you need to start with someone who can teach you how to bake."

"I can't ask you to do that. It wouldn't be fair. You're a teacher, right?" At her nod, he continued, "My younger sister Lynnie is a teacher, too, so I know teachers work longer hours than most people think they do. It's not all long vacations and short days—Lynnie tells me there's marking and assessment and preparation on top of everything at school itself, plus activities after school and at lunchtimes."

She smiled. "That's true. But you're not asking me to help. I'm offering to teach you to bake."

"You'd really do that for me?" He looked surprised.

"Sure." She shrugged. "It'd be the neighborly thing to do. Plus, now you've told me about what happened to Harry and what the First Responders are doing, I'd really like to do something to help with the fundraising."

"Thank you. I accept." He paused. "As long as I can do something for you in return."

She felt herself flush. "There's really no need. It's fine."

"Well, I appreciate it, Stacey." He smiled at her. "Are you sure your boyfriend won't mind you helping me?"

"I don't have a boyfriend." And what a loser that made her sound. If she told him why, she'd sound like even more of a loser. "I'm kind of focusing on my career right now."

"Uh-huh."

The fact he'd asked her that question probably meant she ought to do the same. Even though she hadn't seen Tyler in the apartment block with anyone that looked vaguely like a girlfriend, it didn't mean that he wasn't spoken for. "Um, will your g-girlfriend…" And trust her stutter to come back right now, just when she needed to sound cool and calm and collected. She held her breath for a second and reminded herself to take it slowly. "…mind me helping you?" she finished.

"I don't have a girlfriend," he said. "I'm focusing on getting the gym into a really strong place and looking at my next direction."

Again, she felt the color seep in to her face. Hopefully he didn't think she was fishing or planning to make some kind of move on him. Then again, he'd asked her about a partner first.

"W-when do you want to start?" she asked.

"Tomorrow?" he suggested. "I don't think I can face setting off the smoke alarm again today. I think the rest of the neighbors might forgive me for doing it once, but not twice."

"Tomorrow after school," she said. "And you're not going to set off the smoke alarm."

"How can you be so sure?"

"F-firstly, we're not making a layer cake, we're making cookies. Because they're easier," she said. "And w-when we do bake a cake, we'll use a different size cake pan."

"Is that what I did wrong?" he asked. "Aren't all cake pans the same?"

"Um, no," she said.

He groaned. "I'm such an idiot. I just bought the first pan I saw."

Charles Allman would've had a field day with that one. But Stacey wasn't anything like her father. "You said yourself that you don't cook. How are you supposed to know what to do if nobody ever taught you? You're not s-stupid. That was just a learning opportunity—just like the smoke alarm and the damp dish towel. So now you do know that pans come in different sizes."

His eyes crinkled at the corners, making her feel warm inside. "Now I definitely know I've got the right teacher to help me. You're nice."

"Making someone feel stupid won't help them learn—it just makes them feel bad," she said. "You needed two pans the size of that one, so then the batter wouldn't spill over the edge as the cake started rising and burn on the bottom of the stove. And I'm guessing nobody told you about lining the pan before you put the batter in, either."

"Uh, no. How do you line a pan?"

"Baking parchment. I'll show you," she said.

"And you really need two pans? I assumed you just made one cake and sliced it in half to fill it. Now I think about it, it makes more sense to have one pan for each layer." He groaned. "What age is it you teach?"

"Kindergarten," she said. "But only for half the week. The other half of the week, I work with the children up to the end of elementary school who have special needs. Dyslexia, ADHD, Asperger's, or s-speech..." She almost cringed as she stuttered, hoping he didn't think she was making some cruel kind of mockery of her students.

"Speech and language difficulties?" he asked. "Lynnie says she has a girl with a stutter in one of her classes—and she's Lynnie's favorite student." He paused. "And apparently the girl doesn't stutter at all when she sings."

"Singing helps. It's to do with breath control," Stacey explained. "And practicing speaking s—" she took a deep breath "—slowly, so you're not so tense and that helps you be more fluent."

"That's why you sometimes take a breath halfway through a sentence?"

Now she really did cringe. "I guess it's pretty obvious."

"Not that much," he said, though she knew he was just

being nice.

She could tell him that she was mostly fine when she taught at school, where she knew what she was doing and she knew she was making a real difference to children's lives. She could tell him that she only stuttered badly nowadays when she was nervous or upset about something. But then he'd think her stupid for being nervous about talking to a neighbor—that she was acting more like an awkward seventeen-year-old girl than a qualified teacher who was ten years older than that. Better to say nothing.

"Uh-huh," she said.

"So what do I need to buy for tomorrow?"

"I'm guessing I have more b-baking equipment than you do," Stacey said. "We could do it at my place."

And why did that sound like a tacky innuendo? For pity's sake. She was *better* than this. Of course a man like Tyler Carter wouldn't be interested in someone like her. The important thing here was the fundraising. She needed to focus on that.

"Are you sure you don't mind using your kitchen? I mean…" He gestured to the doorway. "My kitchen right now is a bit on the messy side."

"If you make my kitchen look like it's been hit by a flour bomb, I'll m-make you clear up after," she said, trying for levity.

It worked, because he grinned. Though in some respects that was a bad thing, because that grin was flat-out sexy and made all kinds of thoughts bloom in her head. Thoughts that really shouldn't be there. He was her *neighbor*. She'd only lived in the apartment block for six months so she didn't know him very well—just that he'd taken in a parcel for her a couple of times, and enough to say hi to in the lobby. The fact that he was drop-dead gorgeous... Well, that was none of her business.

"What ingredients do I need to buy for the cookies?" he asked.

"I've already got most of them. I'll just need to pick up some butter on the way home tomorrow," she said.

"I can do that," he said. "How much do I need to buy?"

"A couple of sticks," she said.

"Great. I'll do that."

"Then I'll see you tomorrow for your baking class. What time?"

"When's good for you?" he asked.

"School finishes at three and I don't have meetings after class tomorrow. About four?" she suggested.

"That'd be perfect."

She drained her mug. "Thank you for the..." Cappuccino was a risky word and there was too much chance of a double stutter in the middle. "Coffee," she said carefully.

"Pleasure."

"I'll wash up my mug," she offered.

"No, it's fine. I'm going to be a while cleaning up," he said. "A mug won't make any difference."

"OK. Well—see you tomorrow."

"See you," he said. "And, Stacey?"

"Yes?"

"Thank you. I really appreciate you helping me."

And funny how his smile made her feel warm right from the inside out.

Chapter Two

TYLER THOUGHT ABOUT Stacey all the way through three classes, two personal training sessions, and a pile of admin, the next day. Thankfully nobody seemed to notice that his attention was slightly elsewhere. But this wasn't good. Since Janine had left him, he'd kept all his relationships strictly platonic. And Stacey was his neighbor, which gave him another good reason to keep his distance. Dating a colleague or a neighbor was just asking for trouble when things went sour. The breakup created all kinds of awkwardness way too close to home.

But there was something about Stacey Allman, something warm and sweet that just drew him in. He wasn't sure if it was those wide blue-grey eyes, her heart-shaped face, or her shy smile that attracted him most.

And she intrigued him. Even though she was shy—and Tyler was pretty sure her shyness had a lot to do with her stutter—she'd offered straight away to help him. She was a special-needs teacher, meaning she had a job where she made a real difference to the lives of kids who needed extra help.

She was *nice* as well as pretty. He didn't understand why she was single. Why on earth hadn't she been snapped up from her very first day at college?

Though it was none of his business and he wasn't going to embarrass her by asking.

She'd asked him to pick up a couple of sticks of butter from the store before their baking lesson. He didn't have a clue what other ingredients she was using, but he was pretty sure she'd refuse any offer of reimbursing her. So maybe he could make it up to her another way. He chose a bunch of flowers from the store—simple, bright yellow flowers that he hoped she'd like—and then called in to Sage Carrigan's chocolate shop to pick up some of her famous dark chocolate salted caramels. Judging by the way Kelly in his team at the gym talked about them, they'd be a more than acceptable thank-you gift.

He dropped off his briefcase at his own apartment, then at four o'clock sharp he knocked on Stacey's door.

She opened the door wearing jeans, a thin white knit sweater, and a gray cardigan. "Hi." She gave him another of those shy smiles.

"Is it still OK to do the baking?" he asked.

"As l-long as you remembered to pick up the butter," she said. "Otherwise it might be a little tricky."

He held up the brown paper bag containing the butter. "A couple of sticks, you said."

"Uh-huh."

"And these are for you." He handed her the flowers.

She looked shocked, as if she wasn't used to people treating her like this, and then color stole into her face, making her look even prettier. "Thank you. They're gorgeous. I love y-yellow flowers—they always make the day feel full of sunshine."

He liked the fact he'd pleased her. Which again wasn't a good thing; he wasn't supposed to be thinking of her in *that* way. Stacey Allman was his neighbor, would hopefully become his friend, and was the woman who was going to save his bacon in the Bake-Off. He needed to keep that in mind.

"Come in," she said, and ushered him inside.

Her apartment had the same layout as his own, but it felt totally different. His own living room was fairly Spartan, with wooden floors and a big leather couch and a big TV he used to watch sports. Hers was carpeted, the sofas were smaller and had plenty of cushions, and her TV was much smaller. Behind the sofa was a large bookcase, and there were pretty watercolors of Flathead Lake on the wall, with the snow-capped mountains reflected in the clear water. The walls were painted primrose rather than plain white, and Tyler was surprised by how much cozier it made the room feel.

And her kitchen was definitely a proper cook's kitchen. There were pots of herbs on the windowsill, a spice rack with jars that clearly got used instead of just being there for display, and she'd set out the rest of the ingredients for the cookies on the countertop, next to a bowl and cookie sheets and measuring cups.

"I'll put the flowers in water first. Then can I m-make you some coffee?" she asked. "Sorry—I only have a French press, not a fancy machine like yours."

"That's fine," he said.

"B-black, no sugar, right?" she asked.

"Yes, please." He looked at the ingredients laid out on the countertop. "I need to reimburse you for those."

"There's no need." She shook her head. "Consider it p-part of my contribution to the fundraising."

"I had a feeling you might say that," he said. "So I brought you these to say thank you." He fished in the brown paper bag and handed her the chocolates.

Her eyes went wide as she recognized the packaging. "Thank you, but you really didn't need to do that."

"I wanted to," he said simply. "You're saving me from making a total fool of myself in the Bake-Off, so this is the least I can do to say thank you. And Kelly on my team raves about these, so I'm hoping you'll like them."

"I do. Everyone loves Sage Carrigan's salted caramels," she said. "Are you telling me you've never tried one?"

"I eat out a lot," he said, "but I don't tend to buy candy."

"This isn't candy. This is…" She stopped, and blushed deeply.

"Go on," he said intrigued.

"My friend Tara at school calls it s-sex on a stick," she said.

Tyler grinned. "Either your friend Tara isn't seeing the right kind of man, or I'm missing out on something."

And then he regretted teasing her because she went all shy on him and turned away, busying herself with switching the kettle on, shaking coffee grounds into the French press, and then putting the flowers in water.

"Can I do anything to help?" he asked.

"No, it's all right," she said.

It wasn't, quite; there was a slight awkwardness between them.

So did that mean that Stacey, like him, felt this weird pull of attraction? Was she, too, flustered by it?

Though it'd be dangerous to speculate. He needed to get the conversation back on to a safe track. As in the reason why he was here. The Bachelor Bake-Off. "So what are we baking?" he asked.

"Choc chip cookies. I have a f-failsafe recipe. It's easy and it helps get kids talking to you."

"You bake at school?" he asked, surprised.

"No. I make the cookies here and take them in. They're useful in meetings, too. They break the ice and kind of make people n-nicer to deal with." She finished arranging the flowers and making the coffee.

"Meetings?"

"Sometimes with health professionals, sometimes with

parents," she said, and turned her attention to the kettle. "I assess the children at our school who we think have special needs, and liaise with the department of education to set up an individual education plan for them. Cookies always help to sweeten the mood of the meeting and they seem to make people listen a bit harder."

"Got you. Some meetings are easier than others," he said, accepting a mug of black coffee. "Thanks."

"You're welcome."

And he'd also noticed that she wasn't stuttering when she was talking about her job. This was a topic where she clearly felt confident enough for her words to flow freely. He wanted her to relax with him, so he'd keep her talking about work for a while longer. "So the individual education plan— that's tailored to help the child's specific needs?" he asked.

"Yes. We aim to include everyone in mainstream lessons as much as possible, but some children need specialist speech and language therapy and that needs to be done in a separate room," she said. "And other children need a helper in class with them—say if they have ADHD. The helper will know the point when the child's had enough and can't concentrate anymore, so the child needs to go and run around outside for a few minutes, then they can come back in to lessons and carry on calmly."

"That sounds like my one-to-ones at the gym," he said. "I can tailor the session to whatever my client wants—I look at what they want to achieve, what kind of exercise they enjoy doing, and the best way for them to reach their goals, whether it's losing weight or toning up or training for something specific, like a marathon or a triathlon."

"We have a lot in common, then." She gave him another of those shy smiles.

And how odd it was that it felt as if the sun had just come out. "Uh-huh," he said. "So this recipe is easy, then?"

"Really, really easy," she said. "Do they give you a recipe you have to follow at the Bake-Off?"

"No. Apparently we can use any recipe we like," he said.

"Then let's give this one a try and see how you do with it." She handed him an apron.

He looked at it. "Seriously?" Then he remembered the mess he'd made in his own kitchen, the previous day. "You have a point," he said.

And at least nobody at work would see him wearing an apron covered in pink hearts. Stacey wasn't the kind of woman who'd take a mean, sneaky snap on her phone and spread it all over social media along with a heap of mockery.

His slight discomfort must've shown on his face, because she asked, "Maybe I should've bought a plain navy apron for you?"

"My sister would tell you off for assigning gender to clothes," he said with a smile.

"I g-guess."

Oh, great. He'd managed to make her nervous again. "I was, um, teasing."

She went pink. "I know. I've been told I d-don't have a good sense of humor."

For a second her eyes looked haunted, and he wondered who'd told her that. Especially as from what he'd seen it wasn't true. "And mine's a bit childish, so that'll make us even," he said. "I have a weakness for puns. The cheesier the better."

"Well, I'll Brie surprised," she said.

He loved the fact she'd made the effort to make a pun, and the fact that it literally *was* cheesy pleased him even more. He grinned. "Nicely done, Miss Allman. Now tell me what I have to do."

She seemed to regain her confidence with him. "We'll start with putting the stove on at 375. You need to preheat the stove so it's hot enough before you put the dough in to bake."

"Right." So far, so easy. "Now what?"

"Line the sheets with baking parchment. That means it's easier to get the cookies off the sheet when they're baked, so they can cool."

Again, it seemed relatively simple. He picked up the roll of baking parchment, tore off a wide enough strip to line the cookie sheet, and she gave him a smile of approval that made him feel warm right to the center of his being.

Crazy.

He wasn't supposed to be thinking of her like that.

"Now what?" he asked, to cover his confusion.

"You need to put two sticks of butter, half a cup of granulated sugar, and a cup of brown sugar into a bowl."

She'd put a table knife next to the measuring cup set. "So that's level measurements?" he guessed.

"Yes."

He followed her instructions. "Now what do I do?"

"Use the wooden spoon to cream the mixture together."

Which meant nothing to him. He had a go at mixing the stuff together, but it didn't look very neat. There were clumps of just butter in places, and lumps of brown sugar in others.

"Like this," she said, and took the wooden spoon from him. When her fingers brushed against his, it felt like an electric shock. He hadn't been this aware of a woman in a long, long time.

She stirred the sugar and butter together, and under her hands the final result looked like smooth toffee. "The idea is to put air into the mixture—not too much, because you want a slightly denser dough with cookies. It's a better conductor of heat, so the butter and sugar melt faster and the cookies go thinner."

He liked the fact that she explained the science behind it.

"Now beat in two eggs and a quarter teaspoon of vanilla extract."

He made a mess of cracking the eggs and had to fish bits of shell out of the bowl. And then he stared at the mixture in dismay. "Is it meant to look like that?" he asked. It looked more like the kind of mistake that you'd scrape straight into the bin rather than put in the stove.

"It's fine," she said. "Now add two bags of chocolate chips and a teaspoon of baking powder."

And then it looked like a mess with added chocolate chips. No way would it ever become cookies.

"And finally four cups of all-purpose flour," she said.

Quite a lot of the flour ended up on the countertop instead of in the bowl.

"It's OK to use your hands," she said.

And suddenly his mouth went dry. *Use your hands.* He had the strongest vision of his hands stroking her bare skin. Exploring. Discovering where and how she liked being touched...

"Tyler?"

He really hoped what he'd been thinking about hadn't shown on his face. The last thing he wanted to do was to scare her away. "Sorry. It still looks... Well..."

"Did you ever make mud pies when you were a kid?" she asked.

"Yep."

"Then treat the cookies as if they're a mud pie."

To his surprise, when he did so, the mixture actually came together and looked like something resembling dough.

"So now I have to get a rolling pin or something?" he guessed.

"Nope." She smiled at him. "That's why I said this is a

failsafe recipe. All you have to do is put spoonfuls of dough on the parchment. Space them out so they've got room to spread—though these ones don't spread that much and they look more like rock cakes than cookies." She smiled. "So then you just close your eyes and taste one."

Tyler really had to rein his imagination back, then. The whole idea of closing his eyes and tasting her mouth…

No.

She wasn't flirting with him. She was being kind and neighborly. And he needed to get a grip.

He forced himself to concentrate on putting the dough onto the parchment. "Like this?" he checked.

"Perfect. Then put them into the oven for ten minutes." She showed him how to set the alarm on the stove.

"Another coffee?" she asked.

"That'd be great—thanks. Can I help?"

"Just sit and talk to me," she said, gesturing to the bistro table at the other end of the kitchen.

He knew so little about her. "So are you from Marietta?" he asked. He didn't remember seeing her at school, but she was a couple of years younger than him so that probably wasn't so surprising.

"No—I grew up in Bozeman, but my mom's sister Joanie lives here and I used to visit with her in the summer. And when I saw the job advertised at the elementary school here, she said she thought I'd be happy here, and I could stay with her until I found my own place."

Which sounded to Tyler as if she hadn't been happy where she'd been living before. With her parents? Because he also hadn't seen any photographs of her with an older couple in her living room, and he had a feeling that Stacey Allman was definitely the sort of woman who liked having photographs of her loved ones around.

"Are you from Marietta?" she asked.

"Yes. I grew up here. I did live in Bozeman for a few years after I graduated, but I didn't really enjoy city living. I prefer living in a small town where most people know each other." He grimaced. "Though I know some people find that claustrophobic." Janine certainly had. And he hadn't been enough to make up for that or, when their relationship had hit that final crisis, to make her want to stay.

He'd found comfort in having people he knew around him, but she'd found it stifling. She'd hated being asked how she was. And, after her last day in Marietta, he could understand that answering would've been too painful—the lie that she was fine would've broken her in the end, and the truth… The truth would've led to all the concern and neighborliness that she'd found so difficult.

"You've always been a personal trainer?" Stacey asked.

"Pretty much. I majored in sports science at university," he said, "and I knew I wanted to work with people to help them achieve their goals. So whether it's a young guy who wants to build his strength or an older person who wants to improve their flexibility or help manage joint pain, I can design the right exercise program to help. I started out training people in their own houses and ran a few classes in the school gymnasium, and then I had the opportunity to buy the building next to the Wolf Den here. So I moved back and set up the gym, and gradually built up my business here."

"That sounds like a lot of hard work and dedication."

"It took time." And he knew he was guilty of using work to shy away from the things he hadn't wanted to face in his personal life. It took two to break a relationship, and instead of supporting Janine properly after she'd lost the baby, he'd buried himself in working at the gym and being involved with the town—two things that had been pretty much guaranteed to drive her away.

"Coffee," she said, bringing over two mugs and coming to sit with him.

"So did you always want to work with kids who had special needs?" he asked.

She nodded. "I guess because I've been there myself and I wanted to make a difference. To help kids before their self-esteem starts getting really low."

"Until they're diagnosed, they must wonder why they're struggling in class when their friends aren't," he said.

"And it's harder still in cases where their parents refuse to accept that anything might be wrong," she said. "That's when a child's self-esteem really reaches a low point."

That, together with her earlier comment, sounded like

personal experience talking; but asking her straight out felt like prying. "So the work you do helps with their self-esteem?"

"I hope so," she said. "But sometimes it takes a while to get a diagnosis. Some kids even get to high school before they start getting the help they really need. They're the ones I can't help and I wish I could."

It was like a lightbulb switching on in Tyler's head.

"I've been thinking about the direction I want the gym to go next," he said. "And I think you've just shown me."

She looked surprised. "How?"

"Running classes at school," he said. "We already work as advisors to the middle and high schools for the student athletes. Maybe I could do some work with the kids who aren't athletes—they'd really benefit from it. Taking part in sports isn't just about the physical stuff. There's a big mental element, too, as people realize they're getting fitter and stronger and they can see what they've achieved. It's why I ask my clients to keep a workout diary. Maybe I could do something for the kids who need a confidence boost."

"Like my special-needs kids?" she asked.

"I hadn't thought about working with specific groups," Tyler said, "but, yes, I could tailor activities for different groups of kids."

"Though some kids find sports really hard." She grimaced. "I could never do anything at school that involved a ball. I'd drop it, miss a catch, or pitch so b-badly that the other team would get easy points and the rest of my team would hate me for it—and don't even ask me about racket sports." She shuddered.

"What about running or swimming?" he asked.

"I hated both of them. I'd always curl up with a book instead, if I got the chance."

"But if someone could show you how to do things you didn't think you could do, and then you actually did them— what then? It'd help you believe in yourself, wouldn't it?"

"I guess. Like you learning how to make cookies," she said.

"Exactly. It's all about technique." He paused. "I need someone who could help me put a proposal together. And if I'm to develop something for kids with special needs, I need input from someone who understands about those needs." He looked her straight in the eye. "I think we'd make a good team."

She blushed. "I don't know anything about sports."

"You don't need to. I can handle that side—but I need to know what kind of issues the kids are likely to have, so I can work out the best way to help them feel they've achieved something. And that'll feed in to their self-esteem—if they feel better about themselves physically, it'll help them in other situations."

"I guess," she said thoughtfully.

And if he could help the kids, he could maybe help her as well. That comment she'd made about low self-esteem had really stuck with him. He could definitely do something about that—a kind of payback for the help she was giving him. But he'd need to approach this carefully, so she didn't feel he was patronizing her or treating her like a charity case. Because that wasn't how he thought about her, at all. "Think about it," he said. "I could run classes after school—in the high school itself, or maybe at Harry's House."

"What sort of classes?"

"Boxing," he said promptly. "Which isn't me teaching them how to fight or to hit people. It's teaching them about strength and agility and discipline. How to move safely and feel strong."

"Uh-huh," she said, not looking convinced. She looked as if she was about to say something else when the buzzer on the stove went off.

"Come and check your cookies," she said.

To him, they still looked like misshapen lumps rather than the neat round cookies you'd buy in a store. But when she told him they were perfectly done and showed him how to move the first couple with a palette knife from the cookie sheet to the cooling rack, he took the rest off the sheets. A couple of them broke in the process, but she didn't seem fazed in the slightest.

"Those ones are for tasting," she said. "Close your eyes and open your mouth."

Heaven help him, he nearly wrapped his arms round her. Because that sounded like an invitation to a kiss.

He really needed to get the idea of kissing off his brain.

Keeping himself under super-strict control, he closed his eyes. Then he felt warm cookie touch his lips.

He opened his mouth and took a bite—and it was vanilla-y, sugary, buttery, chocolaty perfection.

"Oh," he said when he'd eaten the mouthful. "I see exactly what your friend Tara means." He opened his eyes and looked straight at her. "Sex on a stick."

She blushed again, and her eyes went just that little bit wider.

So she *did* feel that weird pull of attraction, he thought. The question was—what were they going to do about it?

"She s-says that about Sage's chocolates, not my cookies."

"It describes your cookies, too. Thank you. They're perfect. May I use your recipe in the Bake-Off, please?"

"Of c-course. I'll write it down for you. Though it might be an idea to do a couple of practice runs so you're c-confident baking them—especially as you have to b-bake them in public."

He noticed that she hadn't suggested making them here. And she was stuttering quite badly. Was he making her that nervous? "Maybe I can get you to taste-test them," he said.

"S-sure. I'll just write down that r-recipe for you."

She'd gone all flustered again, he thought as he watched her write. He needed to make a retreat—and then work out how to get her relaxed with him again. Maybe more baking.

Or maybe he could persuade her to help him with the exercise therapy idea. The more he thought about it, the more he was sure they'd be a good team.

"I've already taken up enough of your time this afternoon," he said. "Thank you for your help, Stacey. I'll try baking them on my own—and I'll bring you a sample for quality inspection."

"OK." She put the cookies in a box. "Try these ones on your team at the gym tomorrow and let me know what they say."

"They'll say," he said ruefully, "that I might have saved my ass for the first round, but the pie and the cake will see me going down."

"And you," she said, "can prove them wrong. Because we'll work on the pie and the cake."

He took the box and the written-down recipe from her. "Thanks for this. I'll wash it up and bring it back tomorrow."

"Whenever suits you. I don't need it for at least a couple of days."

Part of him wanted to kiss her on the cheek; but part of him knew it would be too much, too soon. Because it certainly wouldn't be just platonic on his part.

"And I promised I'd clean up after myself."

"It's OK. It doesn't l-look as if you flour-bombed it. I don't mind sorting it out."

She definitely wanted him out of her apartment. Time to

take the hint. He removed the apron. "I'll wash this," he said.

She shook her head. "No need. It'll go in the laundry tomorrow."

Or maybe she didn't trust him not to shrink it or get dye from something else all over it. After all, he hadn't exactly shown much prowess so far with his domestic skills, had he? "OK. Thanks. See you later," he said, and left her apartment.

Chapter Three

S TACEY COULDN'T STOP thinking about Tyler as she cleaned up her kitchen. The way he'd closed his eyes and opened his mouth to let her feed him the cookie...and how tempted she'd been to kiss him, instead. To touch her lips to that beautiful mouth. To taste and nibble and see how she could make him sigh with pleasure.

But what on earth would someone like Tyler Carter see in someone like her?

You're so dumb, Stacey.

Her father's voice again. And she knew that voice was right. It would be much more sensible to keep things platonic between herself and Tyler. Which was why she'd backed off and suggested that he did the practice runs of the cookies on his own, rather than with her. The last thing she wanted was for him to think that she had the hots for him—particularly because she did. Though to be fair, she thought, any woman with red blood in her veins would find Tyler Carter attractive.

She distracted herself by curling up with a mug of hot

chocolate and her laptop, and working on the case file for her newest student. But Tyler's words were still echoing round her head. *Sports can really help with self-esteem... I need someone who could help me put a proposal together. Someone who understands about special needs.*

He'd even said he thought they'd make a good team.

And maybe he was right.

Maybe together they could make a difference. Maybe they could stop some kids feeling awkward and stupid and as if they didn't belong. And if she could stop someone feeling the way she'd felt throughout most of her own teen years, that would be a really good thing.

She could work with him.

But she'd have to drown out her father's voice yet again before she approached Tyler on the subject.

"NO WAY DID you bake these, Ty," Kelly said in the office at Carter's Gym after her first mouthful. "Where did you buy them? Somewhere in Bozeman?"

"I'll have you know, I made them with my own fair hands." Tyler almost—almost—admitted that he'd set off the smoke alarm in his apartment. Except he knew Kelly wouldn't be able to resist sharing that little tidbit with the other trainers, and the news would leak straight over the road to the fire station.

"You really expect us to believe you've developed a sudden ability to bake, when you made such a mess of grilled cheese in the staff kitchen here?" Jason asked.

"Is it so hard to believe?" Tyler protested.

"Yes, it is," Sam said. "So who made the cookies *really*?"

"Seriously—I made them myself."

"All on your own, or with help?" Kelly asked, narrowing her eyes at him.

"With a little help." He could admit that much.

"From?" Jason asked.

"Someone with a much kinder heart than you three," he retorted with a grin, refusing to let them press him into revealing his baking teacher's name. "Someone who wouldn't have tossed me to the wolves and signed me up to bake stuff in public."

"It's for a good cause," Kelly reminded him.

"And I could've donated cash and prizes instead."

"Yeah, but this way you're actually *doing* something," Sam said. "Don't you always tell the clients that making a bit of an effort always pays extra dividends?"

Hoist with his own petard. "And that's why," Tyler said, "I'm making the effort to learn how to bake."

"So does that mean we get to sample the results of your lessons?" Jason asked.

"You might regret that," Tyler warned with a grin, "but yes, it does."

After his shift, he called in to Monroe's to pick up more ingredients before he went home to practice his baking.

Except, even though he was sure he followed Stacey's recipe to the letter, the cookies just weren't the same. The edges were browner and harder—and not in a good way, because they tasted bitter—and the texture just wasn't right.

Where had he gone wrong?

There was one person he could ask. Or was he being too pushy?

Then again, she *had* offered to help. And he'd washed up the container she'd lent him the previous night and needed to give it back, right? He put some of the latest cookies on a plate, tucked the plastic box under one arm and headed next door.

"Oh—hi!" she said, sounding slightly breathless when she opened the door.

"I brought your box back."

"Thank you."

"And I thought you might like to try my first attempt at the cookies on my own," he said. Then he glanced at the plate. "Or maybe I should take these round all the apartments here instead and get people to donate to Harry's House in exchange for me *not* making them try them. They're a bit, um, crispy. In the wrong way."

"It looks to me as if you left them in for about two minutes too long," she said. "Or maybe your stove's not the same as mine."

Not the same? He didn't understand. "A stove is a stove is a stove, right?"

She wrinkled her nose. "Some are hotter than others—even if you've switched them to what you think is the same temperature. If yours is fan-assisted, the food will cook quicker."

"Fan-assisted? How do you know if it's fan-assisted?"

She smiled. "You really don't cook, do you?"

"Nope." He gave her a rueful smile. "And nobody at the gym believed I made those cookies."

She smiled. "Well, you did."

"If I take this batch in, I'll never live it down."

"Either take the temperature down twenty-five degrees, or check the cookies two minutes earlier," she said.

"Got it." He paused. "Would you, um…?" How crazy that he felt like a teenager, all tongue-tied and not sure how to ask her out. "Would you like to have coffee with me?" he finished. "At the Java Café. To say thank you for helping me tonight."

"I haven't exactly helped you," she said.

"You told me where I went wrong. Which nobody else could've done," he pointed out. "So. Can I buy you that coffee?"

"That's really nice of you, but I'm afraid I can't. I'm writing an assessment tonight," she said.

Was she really busy? Tyler wondered. Or was she using work as an excuse because she didn't want to see him?

But then, before he could suggest another evening, she asked, "Do you want me to come next door tomorrow and help you with another batch?"

Perhaps she really was busy, then, and not avoiding him. "If you're not already doing something and I'm not being too cheeky, asking for more help." He paused. "And I'll make you dinner to say thank you."

She raised an eyebrow.

Fair enough. He wasn't actually going to cook it himself. "OK, I'll order in dinner," he amended. "Do you like Italian? Rocco's has a great delivery service."

"Only if we g-go halves."

It was a start. "OK. Halves works for me." He looked at the cookies. "Nobody's going to eat these—I think they're planning to auction off the cookies after the Bake-Off, but I have a feeling they'll have to get people to bid *not* to have to take these."

"You could still make your team eat them. Tell them you need them to support your efforts, as they're the ones who signed you up," she suggested.

He grinned. "You have an evil streak, Miss Allman. I like it." He lifted his hand to high-five her. She looked faintly wary, but pressed her palm against his.

Again, it felt as if electricity zinged through his skin where it touched hers. He hadn't reacted to anyone like this in a long, long time.

"Tomorrow," he said, and cringed inwardly at the fact that his voice had gone slightly husky. Hopefully she hadn't noticed. The last thing he wanted to do was to scare her off.

"What time's good for you?"

"Six?" she suggested.

"Great. I'll order takeout for delivery at seven," he said. "What's your favorite pizza?"

"Margherita with mushrooms and spinach," she said.

No pepperoni? Well, OK. He could live with that. And actually he quite liked that she added greens to pizza. "Mushrooms and spinach. And dough balls?"

"That'd be good. Tomorrow, then," she said. "Let me know how much I owe you for my share."

STACEY SPENT THE whole of the next day thinking about Tyler. He'd already bought her flowers and chocolates to say thank you for helping him. He hadn't needed to buy her dinner as well. Or did that mean he liked her and wanted to get to know her better?

So dumb...

"No, I'm not d-dumb," she said out loud. "I'm hearing-impaired and I have a stutter. I'm shy and a b-bit awkward. But I'm not dumb."

Even so, there were butterflies doing a stampede in her stomach when she knocked on Tyler's door at six. This wasn't a real date, so why did it feel like one? And why did she think she was going to mess it up?

He gave her the warmest, sweetest smile. "Hey. Come in.

Cappuccino with a spoonful of sugar, right?"

"Thanks, that'd be lovely."

"Come and sit in the kitchen with me," he said, and made the coffee.

She accepted the mug gratefully. "Thanks."

"Had a good day?" he asked.

"Yes, thanks. You?"

He smiled. "Great."

"So did you make your team eat the cookies?" she asked.

"I did. And let's just say this time they believed I made them all on my own," he said with a grin. "But they were brilliant about it—they ate the cookies to be supportive. Even though they had to dunk them in coffee first before they could choke them down."

She grinned back. "Tomorrow you can wow them again, because this batch will be better."

"So you're going to talk me through it?"

"No, you're going to talk me through it," she corrected. "I guess it depends on whether you're a visual learner, an auditory learner, or a kinesthetic learner."

"Respectively that's learning by seeing, hearing or…I'm guessing doing?" he asked.

"Spot on. Most people are a mixture."

"I think I learn by doing." He looked thoughtful. "So let's go. First, I cream the butter and sugar," he said, then showed her the end result.

"Perfect," she said.

"Add the baking powder, egg, chocolate chips—and it's meant to look as if a dog's just thrown up in the bowl."

She laughed. "It's not that bad."

"Add the flour, and squidge it together as if I'm making mud pies," he said. "Then spoon it on to the cookie sheet."

And he was doing all this without referring to the sheet of paper on the countertop. "If you paid attention like that in your lessons at school, you must've been every teacher's favorite student," she said.

"Except art, because I can't draw a straight line with a ruler. And history and geography," he said, "because I only really listened to the teachers I liked."

Stacey went hot all over. Was this Tyler's way of saying that he liked her, because he'd listened to what she'd told him? To stop herself thinking ridiculous things, she asked, "Did you put the stove on?"

"Ah—no. So it needs how long to warm up?"

"About fifteen minutes."

"OK. But I can still put the cookies on the cookie sheet while I'm waiting for the stove to warm up, right?"

She nodded.

"So I cook them at 375 degrees." He switched on the stove, then concentrated on spacing out the dough so the cookies wouldn't merge into each other as they spread. And how gorgeous he looked when he was focused. His mouth was very slightly parted, and there was the tiniest furrow between his eyebrows. Stacey almost had to sit on her hands to stifle the urge to touch him and smooth away that furrow with her fingertip, then slide her palm down his face, trace his lower lip with the pad of her thumb, and then kiss him.

Her deal with Tyler Carter was for cooking, not kissing, she reminded herself sharply.

"You need to use slightly bigger spoonfuls of dough," she said, "and to put the timer on for two minutes less."

"Got it." He followed her directions, and this time the cookies turned out perfectly. "The team's going to accuse me of buying them in again," he said glumly.

"I can vouch for you," she said with a smile.

"No—you're my secret ingredient," he said.

Thankfully then the delivery boy from Rocco's arrived, giving Stacey a chance to regain her composure.

"Would you like a glass of wine?" Tyler asked.

"I… OK. Thank you."

"Red or white?"

"Whatever you're opening," she said, wanting to keep things easy.

"Red," he said. "I love Italian wine with Italian food."

Stacey still felt slightly shy but she reminded herself that this wasn't a real date; she was just helping him make cookies and they were eating together simply because it was convenient. But her fingers brushed against his when both reached to dip a dough ball in the melted garlic butter at the same time and it sent a shiver all the way down her spine.

"I'm working the late shift at the gym tomorrow night,

but can I take you out to dinner on Thursday to say thanks for helping me?" he asked.

That definitely sounded more like a date, and panic sent her into a flat spin. She wasn't good at dating. She never knew what to say, and then her stutter got worse and her date got embarrassed by her and it all went wrong. "It's fine. You really don't n-need to do that."

"I was thinking maybe we could talk about the other things I'm supposed to bake," he said, "so it's sort of a business meeting."

Of course it was. Just like her father always said, she was dumb. Dumb to think that Tyler would see her in any way other than a neighbor and a sort-of colleague—and perhaps a friend. "OK. And maybe we can talk about the school projects, too."

"Great idea," Tyler said. "We can go to Grey's. They do amazing burgers and even I will eat their sweet potato fries rather than asking them to swap the fries for salad. I'll come and collect you at half-past six."

"OK. And I'd better let you get on," she said. "See you Thursday."

"YOU'VE GOT A secret," Tara said in the elementary school's teachers' lounge on Wednesday lunchtime.

Stacey frowned. "I'm not with you."

"You keep looking into the distance and smiling to yourself. So. What's his name?"

Stacey felt herself flush. "I don't know what you mean."

Tara grinned. "Yes, you do. Your eyes are all dreamy. And don't tell me that it's a pile of paperwork making you look that way."

Stacey sighed. "It's not what you think. I'm helping my neighbor, Tyler Carter."

"Tyler Carter? As in the owner of Carter's Gym and the sexiest personal trainer in Marietta?" Tara asked.

Stacey scrunched up her nose. "You know the Bachelor Bake-Off fundraiser for Harry's House?" At Tara's nod, she continued, "His team at the gym and some of the clients sponsored him and signed him up to be one of the bakers. Except he can't bake."

"And you're teaching him?"

"To make c-cookies. Yes."

"The same ones you bring to school?" Tara raised an eyebrow. "And what's he teaching you in return?"

Stacey felt her color deepen. "Nothing. I'm just helping him out as a n-neighbor and a f-friend."

"You're stuttering, honey," Tara said gently. "Which tells me you don't think about him that way. Just be careful you don't get in too deep."

Because Tyler was way out of her league. She already knew that. "We're just f-friends," she protested. It was true—at least from his point of view.

"Tyler Carter's a nice guy," Tara said. "He was a couple of years above me at school. My entire year group was in love with him. And he was always gallant to all of us—whether we had braces, acne, freckles, bad hair, or whatever else we were cringing inwardly about, he never made fun of anyone or made them feel anything other than special."

So the way Tyler made her feel was just the way he was with everyone? Part of her appreciated that he was a nice guy; but part of her was disappointed. She'd been starting to think that maybe he found her special. Still, better to know now than to make a fool of herself. "Got it," Stacey said.

"He's one of the good guys, so don't think I'm trying to put him down," Tara said. "I'm not trying to spread gossip, either, but I know he's passed up a few offers lately. I don't think he's looking for commitment right now. He was living with someone, a while back, and I think it was pretty serious, but she's not on the scene now."

Stacey decided she'd make very sure that Tyler had no idea what she was starting to feel about him. She'd play it safe and keep it strictly platonic. "Thanks for—well, looking out for me," she said. For stopping her making a fool of herself.

"That's what friends are for," Tara said.

"I'm not g-getting involved with him—just helping with the fundraiser. I was kind of hoping you'd buy a ticket to the Bake-Off and maybe sit with me?"

"Of course I will. We'll get a group together," Tara said.

"And if you need any ideas, I'm your wing woman."

ON THURSDAY NIGHT, Tyler knocked on Stacey's door. "Ready?"

"Ready," she said. Thanks to Tara's warning, she hadn't spent hours on her makeup or wondering what to wear. She'd simply been practical and dressed in jeans, a thick sweater, flat boots, and a coat, because in a Montana winter it was way too cold to wear anything else.

"I booked us a booth," he said.

"Great."

He tucked his arm into hers as they went out into the street. "The temperature's dropped and it's a bit slippery underfoot. I'll stop you falling if you lose your balance."

Which was a nice thing for him to do. He'd do the same for any female between the ages of six and ninety-six, Stacey knew. It didn't mean anything more than the fact that Tyler Carter had really good manners. How crazy that it still made her feel cherished.

"It's so pretty in Marietta when it snows," she said, to cover her confusion. "I love the way the store-f-fronts are lit up and the sidewalks have a sprinkling of snow."

It was also incredibly romantic. But Tyler Carter wasn't looking for romance. He was looking for friendship, for someone to help him make a difference to the world. She could do that; she just had to keep reminding herself that friendship was all that he was offering.

As they walked down Main Street, she could see Grey's Saloon on the corner. "And that's one of the prettiest buildings in Marietta. I love the balustraded balcony."

"It used to be the town bordello," Tyler told her. "The girls used to walk up and down the balcony to attract the clients."

"Seriously?"

"Seriously." He smiled at her. "If you like history, go talk to Chelsea Collier—she knows everything about the history of the town."

When they went into Grey's they were greeted with a nod by Reese Kendrick, the laconic saloon manager. "You're in the booth at the end," he said.

"Thanks, Reese." Tyler returned the nod and ushered her over to the booth.

"So you recommend the burgers and sweet potato fries?" she asked.

"And the huckleberry pie is to die for."

"I'm kind of surprised a gym owner would recommend pie."

He gave her one of those knee-melting smiles. "It's OK for me because I burn off a lot of calories during the day."

When the food arrived, she tried the burger. "You're right. This is amazing."

"The food's always good at Grey's. Ry Henderson used

to be the chef here," Tyler explained, "and his red velvet cheesecake was legendary."

"Could he not have helped you learn to bake?"

Tyler wrinkled his nose. "Apart from the fact that he's about to be a new dad, so he's going to have his hands full, he's one of the judges of the Bake-Off."

"So there's a conflict of interest, then."

"Yup. But, thanks to you, I don't have to worry about that." He paused. "You know our project? I've been doing some research today into the studies showing the effects of exercise on self-esteem."

Our project. Crazy how that made her feel warm inside. "What did you come up with?" she asked.

"There's a study showing that lifting weights is really good for your self-esteem—each time you lift a little bit heavier, you feel more capable, and that increases your feeling of self-worth. You can actually measure your progress."

Stacey liked the sound of that; and maybe it was something she could do herself. Though she did have one worry. "But doesn't lifting weights make you—well…"

"Bulk up? Not if you're a woman," he said with a smile. "It just makes you strong."

Maybe she could ask him to teach her.

But that might be pushy.

"I'm referencing all the studies in my report—everything from pregnant women to elderly participants—and the principles are the same, whatever the group. We need to set goals, keep them small and manageable, and help the kids measure the changes, so it makes them feel more confident and capable. So they might be able to run on the spot for ten seconds one week, fifteen seconds the next, and they can measure how much better they're getting."

"So you're thinking aerobics?"

"Probably circuit training," he said, "so it's a bit of everything and if I mix it up that'll keep it fun for them. The important thing is that they keep coming back and keep getting a little bit better every time, so their confidence grows and they start feeling good about themselves. We can maybe start with school—then, once Harry's House is up and running, I can run classes there, too."

"I agree—the teen years are tough, and anything that helps get the kids through them is a good thing." She liked the way he was thinking—and his obvious dedication. "So what do you need from me?"

"I could do with a list of the kind of difficulties the kids with special needs face—and then maybe I could ask you to read over my proposal and see where it needs improving?"

"I can do that," she agreed.

And at the end of the evening she realized that she'd hardly stuttered at all in Tyler's company, because she felt so at ease with him.

How had that happened? It had taken her months with her other friends in Marietta, and even now she felt waves of shyness and self-doubt with them. But with Tyler she just felt good.

Again, he tucked her arm into his on the way back to their apartments. Outside her door, for a second she thought he was going to kiss her goodnight, and her heart rate kicked up a notch.

But then he smiled at her. "I really enjoyed spending time with you tonight, Stacey."

"Me t-too," she said.

"Maybe we can do that again, sometime."

"As friends," she said swiftly, not wanting him to think that she was trying to come on to him.

"Sure." His eyes crinkled at the corners. "I'm on early shift tomorrow, so I'll practice my baking when I get home and bring you cookies after school."

"That'd be good. Goodnight, Tyler."

"Goodnight, Stacey."

As she let herself into her apartment, Stacey had to admit that she was disappointed he hadn't kissed her, even on the cheek.

Then again, there was Tara's warning. Tyler wasn't looking for commitment. She'd just be setting herself up for heartbreak if she hoped they could be anything more than just friends. So it was better to play it safe and keep her heart under wraps.

Chapter Four

FRIDAY WAS A good day at school for Stacey. The assessment from one of her newest students, Rick Blake, had come through from the speech and language specialist, and the boy seemed relieved that finally he had a label to explain why he was as he was. "So I'm not just dumb?"

"You're absolutely *not* dumb," she reassured him, her heart aching for him. She knew exactly how he felt: been there, done that, and her father had bought her the T-shirt. "But you must've spent so long feeling frustrated and angry that you couldn't do the same things as everyone else."

"It's why I acted up at my old school," he confessed. "But you're not like them, here. They just said I was naughty and stupid, and I hated the way they made me feel."

"You're neither naughty nor stupid," she said. "And none of the teachers here in Marietta think you are. We're on your side, Rick. And so are your mom and dad." Thankfully the Blakes had recognized that their boy wasn't lazy or defiant or stupid—that there was a reason why he was struggling at school and getting frustrated. They'd been happy to work with the elementary school to get the best for their son. "We can do a whole lot of things to help you. But I need you to promise me you'll come and talk to me if you feel things aren't going right, OK?"

He nodded. "I promise."

And Tara was there at lunchtime in the teachers' lounge with a ready smile. "How are the baking lessons going?"

"OK." Stacey wasn't ready yet to talk about the other project. Not until she'd really discussed it with Tyler.

"I've talked to the other teaching assistants, and we're all coming to the Bake-Off with you," Tara said.

"Great. It's $10 a ticket, and the first round's at Marietta High on February 4," Stacey said. "They have stalls, refreshments, and a raffle, and the cookies are being auctioned off in lots of a dozen afterward."

"Sounds good. And all the bakers are bachelors, I hear?"

"You'd have to ask Jane McCullough," Stacey said with a smile. "All I know is what Tyler told me."

"Hunky bachelors baking cookies. Works for me," Tara said with a grin. "If I collect the money from everyone and get it to you on Monday, can you organize the tickets for us?"

"Absolutely," Stacey promised.

But her day took a dip after school when she went to pick up a prescription for her aunt Joanie from the pharmacy on Main Street.

Carol Bingley, the pharmacy owner, was at the counter.

Stacey tried to avoid Carol whenever she could because Carol always seemed to think the worst of people and was very forthright with her opinions. Today, Stacey had no choice so she simply smiled and said, "Good afternoon, Mrs. Bingley. I've come to collect my aunt Joanie's prescription. How are you?"

She was horrified when, instead of replying with a similar pleasantry, Carol said, "So you're seeing Tyler Carter, then?"

"I…" Stacey was too shocked by Carol's accusatory tone to deny it quickly enough.

"His last girlfriend really didn't work out. She'd had enough of him and hightailed it out of Marietta."

This was the kind of gossip Stacey really didn't want to hear.

Carol handed over the prescription. "Just you be careful. Word to the wise." She tapped the side of her nose. "That's all I'm saying."

Something about Carol's tone reminded Stacey of her father at his most unkind and she just saw red. She knew nothing about Tyler's last relationship and it was none of her business, but the man she was getting to know was a decent man, kind and thoughtful, and she didn't like the way Carol was insinuating that Tyler had driven off his last girlfriend. Sure, Tara had warned her off, but she'd been very clear that Tyler was one of the good guys—he just didn't want commitment.

"I'm n-not his girlfriend," she said. "I'm his neighbor.

He's a good man. He's trying to do something nice to support Harry's House and I'm h-helping him."

Carol looked taken aback. "But you had dinner with him in Grey's last night."

How on earth did the woman know that? Did she have a spy network covering the whole town? But Stacey was too angry to be upset at the invasion of her privacy. "Actually, we were t-talking about what he's going to cook in the B-bake-Off," Stacey said. "So as I've raised the subject, maybe you'd like to give a donation or b-buy a ticket to the event. B-better still, *both*."

Carol blustered, "Well, I'm sure…"

"Good," Stacey cut in, not giving Carol a chance to wriggle off the hook. "I'll ask Tyler to tell Jane McCullough to come and see you for a donation and to sell you a t-ticket. Thank you for my aunt's prescription. I look forward to seeing you there."

She was still fuming by the time she'd reached her aunt's.

"What's happened?" Joanie asked. "Have you had a fight with your dad?"

"I haven't spoken to Dad for a month." Stacey had wriggled out of making phone calls recently by simply sending brief, cheerful texts to stay in touch with her parents. That way, all communication stayed amicable and her father didn't have a chance to put her down or make her feel bad. "It's Carol Bingley. She's so mean-spirited."

"Take whatever she says with a pinch of salt, honey. Everyone else does," Joanie advised. "Sorry. I feel bad now. If I hadn't asked you to pick up my prescription, you wouldn't have—"

"It's fine," Stacey said, "and I don't mind picking up your prescription. It's the least I can do, after what you did for me."

"Now, Stacey, honey. I just did what anyone would've done."

More like what her own parents should've done, but hadn't. "You made a difference for me," Stacey said, "and now it's my turn to do something for you. Your knee's worse in this weather and I don't want you slipping over in the snow and hurting yourself."

"You're a good girl," Joanie said. "You know, I always wish you'd been mine."

So do I, Stacey thought, and patted her aunt's shoulder. "Hey. Now let me make you that cup of hot chocolate."

WHEN TYLER CAME round to her apartment with cookies later that afternoon, this time the dough wasn't quite cooked.

"Some people like their cookies super-soft, but I think the judges would tell you that these ones needed a couple minutes more in the stove," she said.

"Ah—I forgot you said either turn the temperature down

or cook them a couple minutes less."

"And you did both?" she guessed.

"Yes." He looked at her. "You look a bit upset—is everything OK?"

"Just a stupid run-in with Carol Bingley in the pharmacy this afternoon when I picked up my aunt's prescription." But seeing Tyler reminded her of how angry she'd felt on his behalf. "You know, I think I'd rather drive to Livingston or thirty miles over mountain roads to Bozeman than b-buy anything from her again."

"Ah, Carol Bingley." He wrinkled his nose. "Don't take her too much to heart. Let whatever she says just roll over you."

Pretty much what her aunt had said. But Stacey couldn't understand the pharmacy owner's mindset. "Why does she always seem to see the worst in people?"

"I think because she's a bit lonely and unhappy, and in her situation sometimes it's harder to see the good in life at all, let alone in people," he said.

"I guess." As his words struck home, guilt flooded through Stacey. Hadn't she just done the very thing she hated people doing with her special-needs children and judged Carol without knowing the full circumstances? "Maybe I was a bit harsh with her."

"What did she say?"

Stacey shook her head. "Never mind, but she implied I was your g-girlfriend, just because we had dinner at Grey's.

She jumped to conclusions and started spreading it round."

"Is it the gossip that's the problem," he asked mildly, "or the idea of being my girlfriend?"

Oh, help. If she said it was the idea of being his girlfriend that bothered her, it would sound rude and obnoxious—and it also wasn't true. But if she said it was the gossip that bothered her most, he'd guess there was more to it than what she'd said—and she didn't want him thinking that she was prying into his past. Plus she didn't want him thinking she was getting ideas about him. This was getting complicated.

"I just don't like people making judgments," she prevaricated.

"Was she judging you?" he asked.

She grimaced. "Can we talk about something else?"

"She was judging me, then."

She frowned. "What makes you say that?"

"Because if she'd judged you, you would've said so when I asked you straight out. Which means, logically, she must've said something about me."

Stacey wasn't going to tell an outright lie. She sighed. "She told me to be careful about you."

"Uh-huh. Well, there are people outside the gym who can vouch for me. Try the fire crew. They might tell you my circuit classes are nasty, and sometimes they hate me the next day when they discover muscles they've forgotten about. But that's why they come and train with me in the first place, because they know I'll push them." He grinned. "One of them'll give me a character reference."

"I don't need a character reference. I think I'm a reasonable judge of character."

He inclined his head. "Thank you." He paused. "Carol probably thinks that at thirty-two I ought to have settled down and married and started producing children, but that's not for everyone." He blew out a breath. "And it doesn't mean I date a string of women and leave a trail of broken hearts behind me, either."

"I wasn't f-fishing."

"I know you weren't." He raked a hand through his hair. "I've got a pretty good idea what kind of things she said. Just so you know, my ex loathed living in Marietta and Carol epitomizes everything Janine hated about a small town—you can't move without people knowing your business and speculating. Half the time they know more about your life than you do, and the other half the time they get it wrong."

So it wasn't Tyler his ex had had enough of—it was Marietta. Carol had got it completely wrong. Funny how that made her feel so relieved.

"But most people in Marietta are nice," she said. "And it's good having people smile at you in the street and knowing who you are, instead of being anonymous in a big city. To have people sharing the good times with you, and being there to help if you're struggling—and to know you can be there for other people when they're struggling."

"That's what I like about Marietta," he said softly. "It's a real community and people care."

"And that's what you're doing right now. Helping people at your gym, helping Harry's House with the Bachelor Bake-Off fundraiser, and starting your new project at the school."

"Trying to." He looked at her. "I'm not working tomorrow. I thought maybe, if you're not busy, we could go for a walk in River Bend Park and talk about the after-school project."

She wondered: was he asking her out on a proper date, this time, or did he really just want to discuss his project? His words and the expression in his eyes were telling her two different things, and she wasn't quite sure enough of herself to know which one was uppermost. Plus there was Tara's warning to take into account. Tyler Carter didn't want commitment, and she wasn't looking for a casual fling.

So she'd take it at face value and assume that he really wanted to talk about the project. "I... A walk would be nice."

"OK. I'll call for you at ten."

"I'll be ready."

"Good." He smiled at her. "See you tomorrow, then."

Stacey thought about it a bit more that evening. So why was Tyler so shy of commitment? Was that because he was still broken-hearted after his ex had left, even though he hadn't been the actual reason why Janine had left? They'd wanted different things; his ex had hated small-town life, and Tyler had said himself that he didn't enjoy living in a city.

Then again, he'd also said straight out that marriage and having kids wasn't for everyone.

Or maybe she was just overthinking things.

It was none of her business anyway.

And they were becoming friends. That would have to be enough.

IT SNOWED HEAVILY overnight; Tyler loved snow, but he remembered that Stacey was used to living in a city. He wasn't sure how long she'd actually lived in Marietta, or how she felt about snow. The tiniest sprinkle on the ground had been enough to make Janine refuse to go out anywhere. Would Stacey be the same? He didn't think she was as high-maintenance as his ex, but his past experience made him wary.

"Morning, Tyler. Um, given the weather, do you still want to go for that walk?" she asked when he knocked on her door.

Meaning that she didn't? "If you don't mind going out in snow, that's fine with me. It just means we might need to wrap up a little more." And then it occurred to Tyler that even if she didn't mind the snow, a city girl might not be prepared for a winter in small-town Montana. Especially if she hadn't experienced it before. "Do you have a hat, scarves, gloves, and rubber boots?"

She smiled. "If I didn't, I'd get pretty cold walking to school every morning."

So she didn't mind snow, then. Good. "Let's go," he said.

He drove them to the other side of town and parked in the parking lot at River Bend Park.

"I never really think to come this side of town," Stacey said, "at least, not for the park. I tend to stick to the park near school if I want to go for a walk."

"River Bend's pretty," he said. "Especially in the snow."

He could see the delight on her face as they walked through the park. "It's like a real winter wonderland," she said. "All the snow on the trees, the river running through the middle, and that huge expanse of white snow. It's gorgeous."

Exactly how he felt about Marietta; and he liked the fact that she could share his joy in the place.

Part of him was tempted to take her hand; but yesterday Carol Bingley had assumed that Stacey was his girlfriend, and she'd been upset about it. He still wasn't sure whether it was Carol gossiping or the idea of being his girlfriend that had upset her most, so he suppressed the urge—even though walking hand in hand with Stacey through River Bend Park in the snow was something he really wanted to do right now.

Instead, he said, "Maybe we could make snow angels."

"Snow angels?" She looked puzzled, as if she'd never heard of them before.

"You've never made snow angels, even as a kid?" he asked.

She looked away. "Mom didn't like me getting m-messy."

In that case, how did she know about mud pies? Unless it had been a one-off that had got her into trouble.

And just what kind of miserable, buttoned-up childhood must she have had, not being allowed to get messy? Every kid got messy at some point, whether it was from doing crafts at kindergarten or running round the park or a garden in the summer. His own mother had never minded. Or maybe he'd just been super-lucky with his parents.

"You're never too old to make a snow angel," he said, and fell backward onto the thick snow with his arms outstretched.

He moved his arms up and down to make the wings, then drew his legs together and pushed them out again to make the angel's "tunic", then carefully stood up so he didn't spoil the outline.

"One snow angel," he said laconically.

"I've never seen that before," she said. "The kids don't do that at school—they make a snowman and play snowballs, but that's as far as it goes."

"Want to try making one?"

She looked nervous.

"You're not going to hurt yourself falling backward," he said, guessing at her fears. A child who hadn't been allowed to get messy had no doubt not been allowed to do anything where she'd fall over and risk scraping her knee, either—and he'd just bet her parents' main concern had been clearing up the mess rather than worrying that their daughter might get hurt. "The snow's thick and will cushion your fall."

"Uh-huh."

"Hey. It's not compulsory," he said, and this time he gave in to the impulse to take her hand. "I used to make these with my sister. I never quite grew out of them."

"Just fall backward," she said, and took a deep breath. "OK. I'll do it."

He could see in her eyes that she was trying to be brave. And how he wanted to lean forward and kiss her and tell her everything would be OK.

Which was crazy.

Instead, still holding her hand, he led her over to a thick pile of snow. "After three," he said. "We'll do the snow angel together."

"One. T-two," she said.

"Three," he finished, and he noticed that she closed her eyes as she fell backward.

"OK?" he asked.

"Y-yes."

She didn't sound too sure. He sat up so he could see her face. "Really OK?"

She opened her eyes and looked at him. "Yeah. I suppose it's like those things you have to do on team-building courses, when you fall backward and have to trust your team will catch you." And then she gave him a brave, brave smile that almost broke his heart, and moved her legs and arms to make the snow angel.

He followed suit, then stood up and reached down to help her to her feet.

"My first snow angel," she said softly.

"It's good. Stand behind it and I'll take your photograph." He took a snap on his phone—and then he couldn't resist a close-up of her smiling. How had he never noticed until now just how pretty his neighbor was?

"Shall we walk a bit more?" he asked.

"I'd like that," she said.

Somehow it felt natural to take her hand. Even though there were two layers of gloves between them—hers and his own—his skin tingled as if she were actually touching him. And he held her hand all the way over to the river and then back to his car.

"Would you like to come in for hot chocolate?" he asked in the corridor between his front door and hers.

"That'd be nice," she said. "And thanks for taking me to River Bend Park. I really enjoyed the walk."

"It's the endorphins," he said. "Fresh air and snow. That's what we need for the kids."

"You're probably right. In winter, at least," she said.

He heated the milk and made two mugs of hot chocolate. "I would offer you a cookie," he said with a grin, "except I haven't baked any yet today."

"Are you confident with them now?" she asked.

"I think so. But I still need to make a pie and a cake. I looked things up on the Internet—but the Internet's a scary place."

"I'll have a think about recipes," she said.

"Thank you." He handed her one of the mugs. "Let's go through to the living room." When she perched on the end of the sofa, he said, "You know what we said the other day about sports? I've been thinking. Maybe I could show you what I meant."

"Teach me, you mean?" She shook her head, looking awkward. "Thanks—it's really k-kind of you to think of that, but I can't ever see myself going to a gym."

If you weren't sporty, the gym could seem really intimidating—full of people who knew what they were doing when you didn't have a clue. No wonder his suggestion had made her tense up and brought her stutter back, Tyler thought. "You don't have to go to the gym if you don't want to. We could run through a routine at my place. Or yours, if you'd rather," he added, wanting her to feel relaxed with him again.

"I..."

"There's no pressure. But it could be fun."

She shook her head. "I'm not good at sports. Sports aren't f-fun for me."

"Not even playing ball with your parents in the park

when you were little?"

"Dad played baseball in minor league. I..." She grimaced. "Maybe if I'd been a boy and I'd been good at sports, we might have connected better."

He frowned. "I don't see the difference between having a son and having a daughter." His own father hadn't made any distinction between Tyler and Lynnie, treating them both the same. "Whether your kids are girls or boys, you still play ball with them, and teach them to swim and ride a bike."

"I wasn't very good at following my father's directions."

In other words, Stacey's dad hadn't been patient enough to play ball with her at the park. Tyler would just bet that Mr. Allman hadn't had the patience to teach his daughter to swim or to ride a bike, either.

She looked away. "Not because I was being deliberately difficult. I didn't hear what he said, most of the time."

He stared at her in surprise. "You're hearing-impaired? Sorry. I had no idea."

"My hearing aids are the in-the-ear sort so you don't see them," she explained.

"Right. So in a noisy environment I need to make sure you can see my face when I talk, and my face is in the light?"

It was her turn to look surprised. "In those situations it helps if I can lip-read, yes. But how...?"

"Did I know? A couple of my clients are hearing-impaired," he said. "I warn them when I'm going to add a new routine at classes, so they can stand in the front row and see what I do."

"That's thoughtful."

"It's what any decent trainer would do. You check if your client has any old injuries or medical problems before you do anything at all with them, and you bear any problems in mind when you work out their training plans," he said. "Just the same way that you assess your kids at school."

"I guess."

"So were you born hearing-impaired," he asked, "or did it happen when you were older—an accident or something?"

"I had tonsillitis a lot as a child," she explained. "The antibiotics affected my hearing but we didn't realize until a long time afterward that the antibiotics had damaged my hearing as well as fixing my strep throat. My dad just thought I was d-dumb or being d-difficult."

Tyler narrowed his eyes at her. "He didn't think there might've been something wrong?"

"No, and I was a bit clumsy when I was little," she confessed, "so I was a bit of a nuisance and he didn't have a lot of patience with me."

He remembered what she'd said the other day about children not getting a diagnosis until late and their self-esteem getting lower and lower. Clearly that was what had happened to her.

"You," he said, "are one of the least dumb people I know. You're a qualified teacher. And you deal with special needs, so that means you've done extra training and you have to work with all kinds of experts as well as kids who need especially gentle handling—and with parents who might not be willing to admit that anything's wrong."

She shrugged. "It's what I do."

"Your dad," he said, "sounds like one of those parents who refuse to see what's in front of their noses."

She shrugged again.

"I take it he realizes now that he was completely wrong about you?"

She winced. "My dad's not very good at changing his mind."

Stacey's dad, Tyler thought, really needed someone to sit down with him, take off his blinkers, and make him see how amazing his daughter was.

"What about your mom?" he asked.

"She's traditional. What Dad says goes."

That, he thought, explained a lot. Stacey had clearly had no support at all from home—except maybe from one person. "And your aunt Joanie?"

"She was a teacher before she retired. She was the one who picked up my hearing problem and got Mom to take me to the doctor," Stacey said.

"I don't remember her at school here."

"She didn't teach here. She moved here with my uncle Peter when they took early retirement," Stacey explained. "She's ten years younger than my mom, and my mom had me quite late."

"So you've got older brothers and sisters?"

She shook her head. "There's just me."

So instead of being delighted at finally having a daughter late in life, her father had been disappointed that his little girl was less than perfect in his eyes—and he'd made her really aware of that disappointment. No wonder she was shy, and that attitude couldn't have helped with her stutter. It was probably the root cause of it, Tyler thought.

And it was something he knew he could help with.

But at the same time he didn't want to patronize Stacey, or make her think that he had a low opinion of her. "Boxing," he said. "That's what I want to do with you. To show you how it could make the kids feel." And how it could make her feel. He knew she was bright enough to work that out for herself. But hopefully she'd take the offer at face value and not think he was trying to patronize her.

"Boxing."

"I'm on the early shift at the gym tomorrow, but we could do the session after work—say at three, if you're not busy?"

"I can do three." She paused. "Do I need to buy boxing gloves or anything?"

"No, I have gloves and pads. Just turn up in clothes that are comfortable to move in, and sneakers if you have them— if you don't, comfortable flat shoes will do. Or even bare feet, as we're going to be indoors." Given she'd said that she hated sports, he doubted she had any kind of special gym clothing, and he didn't want her to feel that she had to go out and buy stuff specially.

"I've got sneakers. Though they've not really been used for a while," she said.

"As long as they fit and they're comfortable, it doesn't matter," he said.

"OK." She finished her drink. "I guess I'll see you at three tomorrow. Thank you for the walk and the hot chocolate."

"Pleasure. See you tomorrow."

Chapter Five

A T FIVE TO three on Sunday afternoon, Stacey stood in front of the mirror in her bedroom and stared at herself. Tyler had said to dress in clothes that were comfortable to move in, but she felt ugly in her ancient leggings, an old baggy T-shirt, and sneakers.

Then she reminded herself that this was for the kids. He was showing her what kind of difference he could make to them. "It's not about you, Stacey Allman," she said, frowning at herself. "It's about making life better for people who've had a rough deal. Don't be so greedy."

When Tyler opened the door to her, he was wearing a form-fitting black T-shirt, black sweat pants, and lightweight training shoes and he looked absolutely gorgeous. How on earth did his clients ever manage to concentrate in his classes? she wondered. She'd end up distracted, mooning over him, and probably falling over her own feet—making a total fool of herself in front of everyone.

"Thanks for coming round, Stacey," he said. "Come through to the living room."

She noticed that he'd pushed the furniture back to make an exercise area in the middle of the room.

"Luckily we're on the first floor of our apartment block," he said, "so we can't upset anyone by stomping about on the floorboards."

"I guess," she said awkwardly.

"First up, are there any injuries or medical conditions I need to know about?"

"You already know I'm hearing-impaired. And clumsy."

"Hearing impairment is no problem—I'll make sure you can see my face, but if you want me to go through anything again or you think you missed something, just tell me." He placed his hand on her shoulder and squeezed lightly, and the warmth of his hand sent a shard of desire all the way through her.

Oh, help. She needed to get a grip. He was doing this as her friend, not her lover.

"As for clumsy—I've never run a class yet where at least one person hasn't gone the wrong way or put their hands up when they're supposed to be down. Nobody's perfect. Including me." Tyler smiled. "Actually, my classes really love it if I mess up the routine while they're still doing it right."

"You mess up the routine?" She blinked, surprised.

"Any instructor who tells you they don't is either an egomaniac or a liar," he said. "We're all human and some- times you get distracted and forget where you are in a routine. The whole point of a class is to have fun and make you feel good."

Which was exactly what the kids needed. "OK. No injuries or other medical conditions," she said.

"Great. We need to warm up first," he said, and went to put some music on. It was a song she recognized from the radio a couple of summers ago, one with a catchy tune and a good beat.

"We're going to start with marching on the spot," he told her.

That was easy enough; even someone as clumsy as she was could do that.

"And then we'll add in a jumping jack," he said, demonstrating it. "Ten marches, one jumping jack."

Counting the steps made it easier for her to follow.

"Ten marches, two jumping jacks," he said, and kept adding in extra jumps until they were up to ten marches and ten jumping jacks.

He smiled at her. "Do you feel warm enough to start the boxing training now?"

"Yes." And she'd just bet that her face was the color of a very ripe tomato.

"Great." He handed her a pair of white cotton gloves.

She stared at them, surprised. "These are for boxing?"

"They're liners for the gloves and it's a lot quicker and easier than wrapping tape round your hands," he said. "The liners soak up the sweat, because your hands are going to get hot. If we didn't make people wear the liners inside the boxing gloves, so we can wash them after every class, within a couple of weeks anyone who came to class would need a peg on their noses before they could even put the gloves on."

If this was his approach to teaching, her special-needs kids would love him. And so would the more vulnerable teens, she thought. "Got it," she said, and put on the white cotton gloves.

"OK." He helped her put the boxing gloves on over the top. "If you were using your own gloves, you'd probably feel comfortable using your mouth to fasten the tapes at your wrist. But for class gloves it's more hygienic if the person using the pads helps the other one put the gloves on. Like this." He fastened the tapes. "Is this OK, or does it feel too tight?"

"It feels fine," she said.

"Good. All right. Next thing is the way you stand. Are you left- or right-handed?"

"Right-handed," she said.

"So you take a step forward with your left foot," he said. "You punch first with your left hand, and then as you punch with your right hand you'll pivot on your right foot so you can follow through—if you don't pivot, you'll hurt your knee." He stood opposite her. "Mirror what I do."

Even though Stacey was pretty sure she'd fall over and make a fool of herself, she surprised herself by managing to pivot the way he showed her.

"Always hold your hands up to protect your face," he

said, "and keep your elbows down. We're going to start with a combination of one-two, and you punch through from your shoulder, keeping your hand up. You're right-handed, so punch one is always your left hand, and then you pivot for punch two."

Again he showed her how to do it and she mirrored him.

"That's really good," he said, and put the pads on his hands. "Now we measure your reach—that way I stand in the right place with the pads up and you can punch as hard as you like without worrying that you're going to hurt me. Extend your arm out as far as you can."

She did so, and he walked toward her until her stretched-out arm just touched the pad he was holding.

Finally they were in position. "This is where the fun starts," he said. "We'll do a few practice punches, and then we'll put music on—I always do my classes to music."

She threw the first couple of punches according to his instructions.

"Good start," he said, "but you need to lift your elbow up a bit more. One-two is a head shot so you're kind of aiming for my face."

She frowned. "I thought you said we weren't encouraging people to fight?"

"We're not," he said. "I'm telling you that so you keep your hands in the right place and you get the most out of each move. You're working smart, this way."

"OK."

She did a few more practice punches, remembering to pivot and keep her elbow up.

"That's good," he said. "Now hit harder."

"But…" she began.

"You're really not going to hurt me, because we've checked your reach and I'm not getting the full force of every punch," he reassured her. "If you just tap the pad, you're not working hard enough. Punch me. Pretend I'm someone who really annoys you."

She thought of her father at his most cutting, and added more force.

"Perfect." He gave her one of those knee-melting smiles. "Now we'll add the music."

She recognized the song as soon as he started playing it: Queen's "We Will Rock You".

"I'll show you how we're going to do it—you know the three beats? You're going to punch in time with them. One-one-two," he said, and demonstrated. Then he grinned. "When anyone from the fire crew does the chorus to this one, I make them do burpees."

"Burpees?"

"Start from a standing position, drop down into a squat, do a squat thrust, and then stand up again." He demonstrated the move, making it look easy, but Stacey had a feeling it was a lot harder than it looked. "But I'll be nice and let you do jumping jacks instead." He grinned. "I have some evil variations. But only for people who ask for them. The whole idea of this is to have fun."

As they went through the song, Stacey found herself feeling more confident. She'd got the rhythm: one-one-two, then jumping jacks for the chorus. When the music ended, she was hot and sweaty. "So that was five minutes of solid punching?" she asked.

"Nearer two minutes," he said with a smile.

It had definitely felt like longer than that—yet, weirdly, at the same time it had gone so quickly.

"I usually start and end my classes with that one, because it's fun," he said.

She thought about it; actually, it *had* been fun.

"Hydration's important," he continued, "so I want you to have some water now." He took off her right glove and handed her a glass; she drank the water gratefully.

"OK? Ready to do some more, or do you want a few seconds' more breather?" he asked.

"I'm ready to go," she said.

"OK." He replaced her boxing glove. "We've done one-two. Now we're going to do three-four," he said. "Instead of punching forward, you're punching to the side, so you'll see I'm holding the pads differently. You still punch with your left hand first. Keep your elbows high because three-four is another head shot—the idea is, if you don't get me with your punch, you'll get me with your elbow as you follow through."

"That definitely sounds like you're teaching me to fight."

He laughed, and she noticed the fine lines crinkling at the corner of his amazing green eyes. This was a man who laughed and lot and found the joy in life, she thought. And she liked that. A lot.

"No. I'm just explaining what the move does if you were to use it in a ring," he said. "We're doing fitness, not fighting. Elbows up."

She lifted her elbow. "This is a bit like a chicken wing flapping," she said thoughtfully.

"Pretty much. Actually, that's a good analogy. Wings down for one-two, and wings up for three-four," he said.

"Chicken up, chicken down."

He grinned. "I'm *so* using that in a class. And I now need to find some music to match. A song about chickens that's got a good beat for boxing. Actually, I'll throw that out as the challenge of the week and my class will *love* it. They'll have a competition among themselves to see who can come up with the most outrageous."

Stacey had always thought of gym classes as serious places, where everyone was perfect and judged anyone else if they got it wrong. She'd tried going to an aerobics class in the city and had been shocked to find that the front row was full of women in full makeup who didn't even seem to break a sweat by the end of the class. She'd hidden in the back row, getting the routine wrong and feeling completely out of place, and she'd had to force herself to go back the following week. When it had been even worse, she'd given up going to the class.

But from the way Tyler was teaching her, she was pretty sure that Carter's Gym would be a very, very different place. Where people knew each other, encouraged each other, and had fun. And where she could turn up dressed as she was right now and nobody would bat an eyelid, whereas at the class in the city everyone had been perfectly coordinated and which designer brand you wore had *mattered*.

"Chicken songs. I'll think about it, too," she said. "Though the ones I know are more for kindergarten—like 'The Fast Food Song'."

"I don't know that one. Tell me," he invited.

"Really?"

"Really."

She sang a few bars, automatically bringing in the actions.

He grinned. "I love it. I could turn that into a workout—I'm going to look it up on the Internet and get a copy for class. But for now we're going to do three-four." He talked her through the move as he did it. "You pivot from the waist as you go between three and four—oh, and you might feel that a bit tomorrow. If you ache when you get up, that's totally normal." He gave her a rueful smile. "Sorry that it might be a tough start to a Monday."

"Uh-huh. Thanks for the warning."

"OK. We're going to take it slowly. One-two, then three-four."

She practiced the moves, slowly gaining in confidence.

"That's great. So now we're going to mix it up a bit. You'll have to listen to the number I call out and watch the pads so you know which punch to do."

Listening and paying attention: two more skills that the kids with special needs and vulnerable teens would find really useful, and dressed up in a way so it'd be fun instead of making them feel out of place or setting up a challenge for them to fail.

"OK. One. One. One," he said.

She'd just got into a rhythm when he said, "Two."

But he didn't seem to mind when she messed up and punched a one instead. "Nobody *ever* gets that right first time," he said. "You're doing great."

Stacey found herself relaxing and actually enjoying it as he challenged her to get the punches right.

"Brilliant," he said. "Time for another water break." Again, he removed her glove and handed her a glass. She took a few sips, and he replaced her glove.

"And now we'll go for the music," he said. "The first one's mainly one-two. I'll call each one, but watch the pads as well."

He put on some more music, and Stacey laughed when she heard the first notes of Survivor's "Eye of the Tiger". "This has to be the iconic boxing song."

"Certainly is." He smiled back at her. "OK, let's go. One, one-one-two, one-one-two, one-one-two."

Stacey was surprised to discover how easy it was to follow and how much she enjoyed it. Every so often, Tyler corrected her, but she didn't feel as if she was a failure. She was learning and getting better and better. He made her stop for another water break after the song, then followed up with Blur's "Song 2" and the Foo Fighters' "Everlong".

Finally, he switched off the music and made her drink some more water. "I think that's enough for a first session," he said. "We'll do some stretching, now, so you minimize the soreness tomorrow." He talked her through a gentle series of stretches.

"So what did you think of it?" he asked when they'd finished.

"Brilliant," Stacey said, and she felt as if she was grinning from ear to ear. "I never knew exercise could be fun like that. It's nothing like the aerobics class I did in the city."

He looked interested. "What kind of class did you do?"

"Just a general aerobics class. I only went twice. I couldn't get the moves right—every time I thought I'd got it, they changed direction and I bumped into the woman next to me. And the women on the front row were..." She wrinkled her nose. "Let's just say I didn't fit in."

He groaned. "Don't tell me—they were all wearing full makeup and designer clothes?" At her nod, he said, "I hate those kinds of classes. I prefer inclusive classes when you have a wide range of people with a real mix of ages and abilities. You teach the moves that everyone's capable of doing, and then variations so that those who want more of a challenge can work harder, and those who need to take it a bit slower can bring it down to their pace. You make sure your routines are sensible, so people can follow them easily. It really doesn't matter if people count the steps out loud. And you never, ever make people with health issues or a slight lack of confidence feel that they're in the wrong place. The way I see it, my gym's for everyone and I'm there to help them get the most out of their time with me."

"Swap health issues for learning issues, and it's the same for me," she said. "You support those who need a little more help, you make sure your middle group is keeping up, and you give more of a challenge to the ones who need it." He'd said before that he thought they had a lot in common, and this proved it. "I think if I'd done exercise like this at school, I might not have hated PE as much as I did."

"Do you reckon our students will like it?"

"The teens will *love* it," she said. "I'm not quite so sure about the little ones I teach—I think they might like things like the jumping jacks a bit more than the boxing, and wouldn't it be difficult to get the right size gloves for them? But if you were thinking about running classes for teens at Harry's House, boxing would be great. I get what you mean now about confidence. Today you've made me feel as if I can do things I never thought I could do."

"Good." His pupils were huge and his eyes looked almost black instead of the sea-green they usually were.

Then he leaned over and brushed his mouth lightly against hers. "You did really well."

Her skin tingled where his lips had touched hers, and she stared at him in shock. Had Tyler Carter really just kissed her?

More to the point, was he going to do it again?

Then he looked horrified and took a step back. "Sorry. I shouldn't have done that."

Well, of course he'd look horrified. They weren't in the same league. He was a nice guy and he hadn't meant to hurt her. It had been a mistake, that was all. She should just brush it off. She opened her mouth, intending to tell him it was fine and she'd forgotten anything had ever happened, but her mouth wasn't working in sync with her brain. Instead she found herself saying, "Why not?"

"Because you're my neighbor. My friend." His eyes looked very dark. "I'm taking advantage of you."

She was going to tell him that she agreed completely, but either the endorphin rush from the exercise had scrambled her brain or her mouth really had developed a life of its own, because she said, "What if you're n-not?"

He took a sharp intake of breath. "Not what? Your friend?"

"T-taking advantage."

There was a deep slash of color across his cheekbones. "So are you telling me that if I kiss you again…?"

She didn't care anymore that she was sweaty and probably looked a mess. Because that look in his expression told her that he wanted to kiss her every bit as much as she wanted to kiss him.

In answer, she tilted her head back slightly in invitation.

He looked her in the eye, stared at her mouth, then looked her in the eye again.

Non-verbal cues weren't going to cut it. She could tell he wanted to hear the words.

"Yes," she whispered.

Then he dipped his head and brushed his mouth against hers. Once. Twice. So very, very slowly.

And it was nowhere near enough.

She took one step toward him, and he wrapped his arms round her, pulling her close to him. She wrapped her arms round his neck, and finally he kissed her properly. Hungrily. As if he'd been starving for her.

When he finally broke the kiss, they were both shaking.

"I've wanted to do that all week," he said.

The idea thrilled her, but she couldn't quite believe it. "I'm n-not even in your league."

"Like hell you're not." He stole another kiss. "You're sweet and lovely and you make me ache." Another kiss. He sighed. "And you're off limits. You're my neighbor. I'm not great at relationships."

So that was it. Rejection. Kind, but still rejection. "Me, neither," she said.

"Maybe," he said, "we could teach each other. You're

teaching me to bake; I'm teaching you to box. And we could teach each other to…" He groaned. "I can't think straight. I know what I want but I can't get the words out." He leaned forward again and kissed her, and it was so sweet that it made her heart ache.

"Yes," she said, shoving Tara's warning out of her mind.

"I want to do this properly," he said. "I want to go on a date with you."

"A d-date." The idea sent a thrill all the way through her.

"Maybe we could go to FlintWorks—I think Lyle Tate might be playing tonight."

"Lyle Tate?" she asked, not recognizing the name.

"He runs the Tate ranch with his older brother Logan and he's a part-time firefighter. He trains in my gym," he said. "You must know him—he's probably the most charming guy in town and he flirts with any female who has a pulse. You can't miss him."

"I've never met him. Apart from going to the book group at the library," she confessed, "I don't really see many people outside the elementary school." Although she'd made friends, she was always aware that she was on the fringes of any group.

"Lyle's a good guy," Tyler said. "Just he's a terrible flirt, so don't take him too seriously."

"Uh-huh." Stacey wondered if this was his way of warning her not to take *him* too seriously, either.

He checked his phone. "Yeah, Lyle's playing at Flint-

Works tonight at eight—would you like to go?"

"I, um, haven't actually been there before. Is it very d-dressy?"

"It's a bar with its own microbrewery—Jasper Flint set it up in the old railway depot," he explained. "I'd say smart casual's fine." He stole another kiss. "If I pick you up at seven, we can have a drink before the show starts, maybe grab some food? The menu there is pretty good."

"I'd like that. Thank you. Though I'd b-better go shower and wash my hair. I'll see you at seven."

"OK." He kissed her again, and then let her rush out of the door.

WHAT THE HELL was he doing, asking Stacey for a date? Tyler thought.

But the way she'd blossomed during his boxing lesson and that wide smile at the end had just done it for him. He hadn't been able to resist kissing her.

And she'd kissed him back.

This could be the worst idea he'd had in years—or it could be the best. Maybe his friends and his sister were right and it was time he moved on from Janine. Maybe Stacey was the one who'd teach him to trust in relationships again: her warmth and sweetness drew him.

Maybe.

AT SEVEN PRECISELY, Stacey's doorbell rang.

"Hi. Ready?"

Tyler looked utterly gorgeous in faded jeans and a burgundy Henley top beneath a thick padded jacket. His dark hair was still faintly damp from the shower, and Stacey's pulse speeded up a notch.

For a second, she wasn't actually able to get the word out. But she took a deep breath and reminded herself to keep this low-key. Yes, this was a proper date—but he'd chosen something relatively casual. It was going to be fine. "Ready," she said.

Tyler drove them to FlintWorks; although he'd told Stacey that the place was a renovation of the old train depot, it still wasn't quite what she'd been expecting. There were big bright paintings on the wall and the whole place felt wide open and airy. There were the steel vats of the microbrewery behind glass walls, a busy open kitchen, and the staff behind the bar were wearing bright blue shirts and friendly smiles.

"This place is amazing," she said. "Do you come here a lot?"

"A fair bit, now I think of it. I do a team night out here on a Sunday night, once a month—mainly because my lot like the buffalo wings," Tyler explained.

He found them a quiet table in the corner with a good view of the stage and, once they'd looked through the menu, ordered them both a beer, wedges, and Cajun-spiced chicken tenders with a salad. And she discovered he was right about the food: it was really good.

Stacey didn't really recognize anyone in the crowd, but several people stopped by their table to talk to Tyler—clearly people he'd known for years or who were clients at the gym—and he introduced her to everyone straight away. She was more used to being on the edges of the crowd rather than part of the center, but with Tyler by her side it felt relaxed and natural to be smack in the middle, and to her mixed surprise and relief she barely stuttered when she answered questions.

One of the bartenders went over to the microphone. "Good evening, everyone. Thank you for coming out on such a cold night. And now I'd like you to give it up for Marietta's own Lyle Tate!"

Amid loud applause, a tall man with sandy brown hair and the most amazing blue eyes walked onto the stage, carrying a battered guitar. Something about his clean good looks reminded Stacey of a young Brad Pitt.

"Good evening. How're you all doing?" Lyle asked, and was answered with whoops and cheers. "I'm going to start with something I think you all know," he said, and launched into Keith Urban's "Somebody Like You".

The crowd clapped in time and sang along in the chorus, and Stacey found herself tapping her foot to the rhythm.

Lyle segued easily to a composition that turned out to be

one of his own, and mixed up some obvious audience favorites in between, from oldies such as "Witchita Lineman" and "Jolene" through to newer tracks such as Dierks Bentley's "Say You Do" and Lady Antebellum's "Need You Now".

Somehow, during the set, Tyler had moved his chair so he was sitting right next to Stacey; his arm was round her shoulders and he was holding her close. She couldn't resist leaning into him. Everything felt really right with the world, and she couldn't remember the last time she'd enjoyed an evening so much.

After the show, Lyle stopped by several tables, chatting to people he clearly knew well, and eventually he came over to their table. "Well, hey, Carter—good to see you here getting a bit of culture for once. Did you enjoy the show?"

"You weren't bad for an amateur," Tyler teased back.

Lyle turned to Stacey. "And how about you, sugar? I haven't seen you around here before. Would you be new in town and needing someone to show you around?"

Tyler groaned. "Stop flirting, Tate. Stacey's spoken for."

"By you? Pity." He gave her a warm smile. "Hey, sugar, I take it you know this guy's about to fall on his ass in another week?"

"How do you mean?" she asked.

"He's in the Bachelor Bake-Off—the fundraiser they're doing for Harry's House." Lyle's blue eyes sparkled. "Given that we heard the smoke alarm in the fire station all the way from the gym's kitchen the last time he tried to make grilled cheese, this is going to be a lot of fun."

Tyler sighed. "I should've guessed. You put up some of my sponsor money, didn't you?"

"Yep." Lyle didn't look in the slightest bit repentant. "As soon as Kel mentioned it, I was in."

"M-maybe we should bet on it," Stacey said. "Tyler's not going to come last."

"How would you know that?" Lyle looked interested. "Unless… Have you been coaching him?" At her blush, he grinned. "Well, then. A bet it is. What are the stakes?"

"T-twenty dollars to the Harry's House fund," she said promptly.

"Make it a kiss as well, sugar, and you've got yourself a deal," he drawled.

She looked at Tyler, who spread his hands. "Hey. Your decision."

"Twenty dollars and a kiss if you win," she said to Lyle. "N-no tongues."

"As if I'd insist on that." Lyle gave her another of those warm, flirtatious smiles that she'd just bet was designed to make any woman's knees go weak; it didn't make her heart beat faster, though at the same time she found herself really liking him. There was no malice in the man at all. He was charming and easygoing and fun.

"I like you, sugar," he said. "You've got a deal."

"Twenty dollars and you s-sing if I win," she added. "My

choice of song."

"Now I *really* like you, sugar. You get bored with Carter here, you come and find me," Lyle said with a grin. "Because I think you and me, we could make some sweet, sweet music together."

She felt herself flush to the roots of her hair. "Um."

He winked at her. "Hey, I'm teasing. I know you're with the gym gorilla. Good to meet you, sugar, and I'm glad you came to the show."

"I enjoyed it. Your voice is g-good," she said.

He swept off his hat and gave her a low bow. "Your servant, ma'am."

When he'd moved on to the next table, she looked at Tyler. "Sorry. I w-wasn't intending to start flirting."

"I don't think you had a choice. Lyle Tate flirts with any female who crosses his path and he makes them flirt back. He was born that way," Tyler said regretfully. "But you don't have to kiss him."

"I made the bet. Just make sure you don't come last. And I'll think of an appropriate song for him to sing. Maybe 'Born This Way'," she said thoughtfully.

Tyler laughed. "I like it." His smile faded. "I like *you*," he said, his voice low and husky and sending a shiver down her spine.

"I l-like you, too," she admitted.

"Good." His smile made her feel warm all over. "Ready to go home?"

"Ready," she said.

Outside her front door, he paused. "I would ask you in for hot chocolate—but I know you've got school in the morning, and I'm on the early shift at the gym."

"It's fine," she said.

"Maybe we can do something together tomorrow evening, even if it's just coffee?" he asked.

She nodded. "I'd like that."

He drew her into his arms and kissed her until she was almost dizzy. "Sweet dreams," he whispered.

And she knew they would be—because they'd be of him.

Chapter Six

TYLER HADN'T BEEN exaggerating when he'd said that she might feel sore the next day, Stacey thought ruefully. Her shoulders ached, and her sides, and a few more muscles besides that she hadn't even known she had. A hot shower sorted out the worst of it; figuring that the aches probably meant the boxing had done her some good, she didn't complain about it at school. But when she answered the door to Tyler that evening, he looked at her with narrowed eyes.

"The way you're moving right now—you hurt, don't you?"

"A little bit," she admitted.

"Where's the worst of it?"

"The backs of my arms, my shoulders, and my sides," she said.

"I can show you a couple of stretches that will help, as well as the ones we did yesterday," he said. "Sorry. I should've said last night."

"It's OK."

"To stretch out your triceps—the back of your arms—hang off the doorframe like this," he said, demonstrating the pose. "Hold it for a few seconds until you find it starts to ease."

She tried it, and was surprised by how quickly it helped.

"For your sides, you need a side bend." Again, he demonstrated; she followed his instructions, and the ache eased.

"How's your back?" he asked.

"A bit stiff," she admitted.

"There's a yoga movement that will help—it's called the child's pose. Kneel down like this, sit back on your legs, and then lean forward until your forehead touches the ground. You can leave your arms by your sides," he said, talking her through it. "Relax into the stretch and you'll find it should help."

"That's better," she said.

"And finally your shoulders." He demonstrated a shoulder roll, which she copied.

"Thanks. I needed that."

"If you'd called me this morning," he said, "I could've helped."

She wrinkled her nose. "We both had work."

"Even so. I'm sorry," he said. "I came to ask—are you busy this evening, or do you want to come and watch a movie with me at my place?"

"That depends a bit on the movie," she said with a smile.

"I'm not so keen on gory ones."

"How about a comedy?" he suggested.

"That works for me."

"Great. What time's good for you?"

"Seven?" she suggested.

"Great." He kissed her lightly. "See you at seven."

Assuming they were still keeping this thing between them low-key, Stacey didn't bother redoing her makeup or changing into a dress. But she did chill a bottle of white wine in the fridge.

"Hey. You didn't need to, but thank you," Tyler said when she went next door and handed him the bottle. He kissed her lightly. "I made us some nibbles."

There was a platter on the low coffee table with a bowl of hummus, strips of pitta bread, carrot and cucumber sticks, and sliced red bell pepper.

She smiled. "That's how I know I'm dating a health freak. Anyone else would've served a bag of potato chips."

He pulled a face. "Empty calories, salt, and saturated fat. No."

"Actually, I prefer hummus and pita." She raised an eyebrow. "I'm assuming you bought the hummus?"

"It's safer than making my own," he said, smiling back. He poured them both a glass of wine, and together they chose a comedy from the movies on his streaming service. And there was something really nice about being curled up on the sofa and laughing together at a movie on a cold winter's night, Stacey thought, with their arms wrapped round each other. No pressure, no worries—she could just enjoy his company.

"Thank you for tonight," she said when the movie had finished and the wine bottle was empty.

"My pleasure. It was good just being with you," Tyler said.

"I guess I'd better… We've got work tomorrow," she said awkwardly. "And I need to finish my book for the book club tomorrow evening."

"Since you're busy tomorrow and I'm on the late shift at the gym anyway, maybe we can go out for a drink or something on Wednesday?" Tyler suggested. "And I need to practice my cookies."

"Wednesday's good for me," she said.

He kissed her lingeringly. "I'll walk you home."

To all of the next door down in the corridor—it really wasn't necessary, but Stacey liked the fact he'd made the effort.

"Goodnight," he said outside her front door, and kissed her again.

TUESDAY NIGHT FOUND Stacey speaking up more than she usually did at the book group; funny how she felt more confident since Tyler had started teaching her to box. And then the conversation turned to the Bachelor Bake-Off.

"A little bird tells me that you're giving baking lessons to one of our bachelors," Rachel Henderson said.

Stacey blushed. How much else had her friends at the book group heard? "I'm just helping my neighbor."

"And, from what I hear, Tyler *really* needs some help," Hannah Phillips said with a grin. "There's a rumor that he once burned grilled cheese so badly in the staff kitchen at the gym that the fire crew heard the smoke alarm from across the other side of the street."

"He's not so bad," Stacey said loyally.

Rachel smiled. "He's one of the nicest guys I know, and he runs great antenatal aqua-aerobics classes. This little one certainly likes them." She rested a hand on her bump. "Ry would've offered to help him out with a few lessons, but as he's one of the judges he has to be impartial." She wrinkled her nose. "I'm glad you're helping him, Stacey."

"Trying to," Stacey said with a smile. "And I'm making some cupcakes for them to sell at the refreshment stall. It's a good cause."

"It certainly is," Hannah agreed.

To Stacey's relief, the conversation turned to Harry's House and what a great resource it would be for the kids of Marietta. But she thought about it all the way home, that evening. Everyone seemed to like Tyler, and yet Tara had said he was wary of commitment. It sounded to her as if he'd been really badly hurt by the woman who'd left him. Had he been hurt too much to trust again? Or could she be the one to heal his heart?

ON WEDNESDAY EVENING, she played pool with Tyler in the back room at Grey's Saloon, on the slightly battered wooden table with its red baize top.

"I thought you said you didn't do sports?" Tyler said, when Stacey had managed a tricky shot that won her the first game.

"Not real sports, but I did play pool at college," she said.

"Why do I get the feeling I've been hustled?" he teased.

She laughed. "Hardly. That was a lucky shot."

"Good enough to mean that I have to buy the next round of drinks," Tyler said, smiling back. "Same again?"

"Yes, please."

They played a couple more games, then afterward they walked home in the snow, hand in hand.

Tyler eyed up the park by their apartments. "Given the way you play pool," he said, "I think your aim might be better than you're letting on."

"Aim?" she asked, mystified.

"We have a park in front of us, covered in snow. Let's see how good your aim is," he said, scooping up a handful of snow and packing it lightly into a ball before lobbing it straight at her.

His snowball landed precisely on target. Although Stacey retaliated, her aim was nowhere as good as his. She missed every single time, whereas Tyler even managed to get one straight down the neck of her coat.

The only way she was going to cover him with snow, she thought, was to cheat. Outrageously.

When his next snowball hit, she dropped to her knees.

"Stacey? Stacey, are you OK?" he asked.

Just as she'd expected, he rushed over to check that she was all right and not hurt. Which meant that technically it was really mean of her to wait until he'd bent down beside her before sitting up and stuffing snow on top of his head and down his coat.

"Oh, what? That's *cheating*, Miss Allman. Your students would be shocked," he said, wagging a finger at her and laughing.

She grinned. "Want to make something of it?"

"Since we're playing dirty, then yes, I do." He pushed her back into the snow, and then kissed her.

Stacey wasn't aware of the cold or the damp starting to seep through her coat. All she was aware of was the way Tyler was kissing her, the feel of his mouth against hers and the heat rising through her body. She wrapped her arms round his neck and let him deepen the kiss.

When he broke the kiss, he pulled her to her feet with a grimace. "Sorry. I got a bit carried away, and now you're cold and wet."

"It's OK. We're nearly home," she said, and glanced at him. "And you're just as cold and wet, too." Especially as she'd shoved that snow down his neck.

She almost—*almost*—suggested that they could warm up in the shower together, but didn't quite have the nerve.

"I enjoyed tonight," Tyler said outside her front door. "Even if you are a pool shark in disguise and you cheat outrageously at snowballs."

"Me, too. Enjoyed tonight, I mean. I am so not a pool shark."

"At least you're not denying you cheated." He kissed her again.

"You're a good aim. I didn't manage to hit you once, so I needed an unfair advantage," she protested.

"Yeah, yeah." He laughed. "I'm on a late tomorrow but I'm on an early on Friday. Do you want to do some boxing circuits and then talk about our project?"

"Yes, I'd like that," she said.

"Good. Friday it is. Shall we meet at my gym?"

Her eyes widened. The idea terrified her.

"After hours?" he suggested. "Say, half-past nine?"

Meeting after hours did make the idea of the place less intimidating. She took a deep breath. "OK. I can do that."

"Great." He kissed her lingeringly. "Goodnight."

"Goodnight." She paused. "And, Mr. Carter?"

"Yes?"

"You look really sexy with snow on your head." She

winked at him, and sashayed through her door.

TYLER STARED AFTER her. Had Stacey really just called him sexy?

OK, so they were dating officially—but he'd really had to hold himself back in the park, after she'd cheated outrageously and covered him in snow and he'd ended up kissing her stupid.

Maybe he should've suggested that they showered together to warm up.

Or that he could be her personal hot water bottle...

He blew out a breath. Slow. That was probably the way they ought to take it.

Though he'd taken it slowly with Janine, and that had gone badly wrong.

Maybe he should try the whirlwind approach instead and sweep Stacey off her feet...

ON FRIDAY EVENING, Stacey changed into her old T-shirt, leggings, and sneakers, and headed next door with two red velvet cupcakes.

"These look amazing," Tyler said. "Is this what you're going to teach me to bake, next?"

"You said pie was the next thing you had to bake," she reminded him. "No, these are a couple of spares from the batch I made for the refreshment stall tomorrow."

"Thank you." He smiled at her. "I would say let's eat them now, but it's not a good idea to eat just before exercising."

"They're both for you anyway," she said.

"Well, thank you." He paused. "Come and see my lair."

Carter's Gym was neat, tidy, and absolutely spotless— and Stacey would just bet that Tyler did his fair share of the cleaning rather than just delegating it to his team. There were various machines grouped together in one area; another area had mats, benches, and racks of weights. And she noticed that the whole wall was mirrored. "Um…"

He followed her gaze. "That's standard in all gyms. It's not from vanity, though I do have one or two clients you could class as the tiniest bit vain," he said with a grin. "It's so you can check your form when you're doing an exercise, and correct yourself if you can see you're doing it wrong."

"Oh." Stacey felt stupid. "The class I went to was in a hall. They didn't have mirrors."

"My studio, where I teach classes, also has mirrored walls," he said. "But it's not to make people feel awkward. My classes usually have a laugh. Come and have a look." He took her through to the studio.

One wall was lined with stationary cycles, and the opposite wall had a rack of dumbbells, steps, and a pile of yoga mats.

"We run a lot of different classes," he explained, "and they're all mixed ability. So some people will use weights so they can work harder, though I advise my beginners and anyone with health issues to stick to body weight exercises. It's all about feeling good, doing the best you can and enjoying it."

She noticed that he'd set out some cones, a trash can, some beanbags, and some different-sized balls, as well as boxing gloves and pads.

"Extra equipment?" she asked.

"I thought," he said, "maybe we could try out some of my ideas as a warm-up."

"Sounds good." She paused. "Tyler, I don't want to put a dampener on things, but this project—it's not just the school principal who needs to agree it. You'll need to get the PTA on board, too, so they can get the parents on board. There will be funding issues to consider."

"My time—or that of my team—would be free. This is *pro bono* work," he said. "And I want to use the equipment that's already there in school."

She nodded. "That makes it a lot more likely it'll go ahead."

"That's another reason why I need your input. You know how schools function," Tyler said, "and where regulations might trip me up."

"OK. So take me through what you're thinking," she

said.

"I want to mix up cardio with exercises about balance and agility," he said. "So we do one cardio, then one non-cardio."

"Sounds good," she said. Though it was hard to keep her attention focused on the project—right now, when he was talking through his ideas, Tyler was really animated and she couldn't take her eyes off him. This was clearly his passion, and it made him light up from the inside.

"I know this is totally the wrong time of year now, but I found a fabulous idea online about setting up a reindeer game. You tell the kids they're going to be helping Santa's reindeer and need to train to help him, so you get them walking over an upside-down bench to pretend they're balancing on a rooftop, do a slalom of cones and say they're weaving in and out of the trees, have to jump between clouds—I'm guessing jumping over hurdles might be a bit much, so we could maybe have colored mats put a little way apart—and then throwing beanbags into a trash can as if you're throwing presents down the chimney."

"That's brilliant," she said. "The really little ones will adore that."

"The important thing is that we make the routine fun for them, so they don't have any idea we're actually doing balance, agility, strength, and coordination," he said. "I could do an Easter bunny thing to start with—we could include bunny hops, and rolling balls across the floor to pretend they're rolling eggs."

"That's a great idea—and we could do a gardening thing, so we can get them to pretend to be different sorts of beans as they move around the room," she suggested. "A string bean with their hands up over their heads, then runner bean and jumping bean are both obvious." She demonstrated the action she'd used when she'd done that kind of thing in her classes. "And they can plant seeds by throwing balls into a trash can."

"We definitely need to record their scores, though—how many beanbags they can get into the trash can in say thirty seconds or a minute," he said, "because then they can see for themselves how much they improve each week."

Between them, they brainstormed a pile of ideas, and Tyler took notes on his phone. "I'll write this up over the weekend and run it by you," he said. "Thanks, you've been brilliant and came up with all sorts of things I'd never thought about."

"You've given me some ideas to use with my classes, too," she said. "Thank you."

He smiled at her. "We make a good team."

The combination of his comment and his smile made her feel warm all over. "Yes, I think we do."

"I did work out a routine we could use for your boxing warm-up," he said.

His enthusiasm was infectious and made Stacey smile for all the right reasons. "Let's do it."

He placed a brown handle on the floor. "For the kids, I'd use a line if there's a court already marked out on the gym hall, or a line of masking tape if not. But you can jump over this for ten seconds."

She did so while he timed her.

"And now…" He tossed a beanbag to her.

She missed catching it, and felt the color seep into her cheeks. "Sorry."

"No need to apologize. You weren't expecting it."

She picked it up. "So what do you want me to do?"

"Put it on your head and walk over to the other side of the room and back—but without it falling off your head," he said.

"OK." To her surprise, it was easier than she'd expected, and she began to relax.

"Ten jumping jacks."

Again, it was easy.

While she'd been doing the exercises, he'd set up a trash can and five beanbags leading away from it, each of them a single big step apart. "Now throw the beanbags into the trash can, from the point where they're on the floor."

The first three were easy; the last two, she missed.

"So now you know your baseline," he said, before she could apologize for getting it wrong. "Ten spotty dogs."

"Spotty dogs?" she asked, mystified.

"You've not done them before? OK. Some people call it a forward crisscross, because that's what you're doing with your arms and legs, and you do it on the spot," he said, and demonstrated the move.

"So your opposite arm and leg go forward and back, right?"

"Right."

Even though her old fears about being clumsy and hopeless tried to sneak back in, she pushed them away and followed his directions, and to her pleasure she actually managed to get it right.

"Great work," he said.

"Why is it called a spotty dog?" she asked.

"I think it's after a wooden puppet that used to be on a kids' TV program years and years ago," he said.

She nodded. "That makes sense."

"All righty." He threw a football to her, and to her relief she actually caught it. "Roll this round your waist while you make big circles with your hips."

"Ten of them?" she guessed.

"Absolutely."

When she'd finished, he smiled at her. "OK. Last one is shuttle runs. You're going from cone to cone, slightly crouched down, moving sideways." He demonstrated it for her.

"Shuttle runs. Ten?"

"Keeps it nice and easy to count," he said with a smile.

To her surprise, Stacey enjoyed it.

"OK. Now we're going to do the whole lot again—

except this time I'll do it with you," he said.

She was laughing by the time they'd finished. "That was fun."

"Good. Warmed up enough to box?"

"I sure am," she said, and he handed her the gloves.

"And I'm going to talk you through what I think I should be doing," she said. "One-two, I punch from the shoulder, I keep my arms up and my elbows down, and I remember to pivot for 'two'," she recited, and demonstrated the move.

"You've got it," he said. "Three-four?"

"I keep my elbows up, so if I miss you with my punch, I still get you with my elbow—and I make sure I pivot."

"What happens if you don't pivot?" he tested.

"I risk wrecking my knee?" she queried.

"Absolutely right," he said. "Let's do this."

He put some music on, and they went through a similar routine to their initial training session. This time, Stacey felt much more confident and she noticed that she made fewer mistakes and he praised her more. But the really strange thing was seeing herself in the mirror. She didn't look awkward and stupid; she looked sweaty, yes, but she looked strong and in control. Seeing herself like that made her feel stronger and more in control, too—and she hadn't expected that at all.

"So how was it?" he asked when he'd done the cool down and stretches with her.

"Good. You're right about the mental stuff," she said. "It's weird, because I didn't expect to feel more confident straight away, but I do. And seeing myself in the mirror—I looked as if I knew what I was doing."

"You *do* know what you're doing," he said. "You did great, tonight."

And she hadn't stuttered at all, this evening.

Not wanting to let herself think about why, she asked, "Did you find any chicken songs?"

"I've got my classes working on it," he said with a grin. "And I've been thinking. You know you said I looked sexy, covered in snow?"

She blushed. "Y-yes."

"You look sexy," he said softly, "when you're all strong and confident and those gorgeous blue eyes of yours are sparkling."

Stacey couldn't remember anyone calling her sexy before. Her few boyfriends had thought of her as a nice girl they could take home to meet their family...until she'd taken them home to meet hers, and then they couldn't have backed off fast enough.

Though Tyler Carter, she thought, might just be a match for her dad.

"Sexy," she said, testing the word out to see if he really had meant to apply it to her.

"Sexy like this," he said, and drew her into his arms and kissed her.

When he broke the kiss, she stared at him. He really had meant it.

"So," he said. "What now?"

"I…" She dragged in a breath. "How about we take things a little less slowly?"

"Less slowly sounds good," he said.

"B-but right now I'm all s-sweaty." And not just sweaty: she was scared she wasn't going to measure up to the ex who'd made him forswear any kind of commitment. "And we're in the middle of your gym. And you have the B-bake-Off tomorrow."

"Tomorrow," he said softly. "Tomorrow night. After the Bake-Off. Maybe we could do something together."

Something.

All kinds of crazy ideas spun through her head.

"S-something," she agreed, flustered enough for her stutter to come back.

He kissed her again. "I'll see you home. And then I'll see you at the Bake-Off tomorrow."

This time, she leaned forward and kissed him. "And then we'll do…s-something."

Chapter Seven

O N SATURDAY, TYLER was working the early shift at the gym so he didn't have to think about the Bake-Off. In theory. Though maybe that was a mistake, he thought, because all his personal training clients wanted to talk about the Bake-Off, and when he was covering the reception desk everyone who came into the gym wanted to talk about it, too.

And all he wanted to think about was Stacey, and the "something" they'd agreed to tonight.

He didn't want to rush her; but, at the same time, he did. He ached for her. And he had a feeling it was the same for her, too.

At least, he hoped it was.

"From this point on," he said at midday, thoroughly fed up with the teasing, "anyone who says the B-word in the gym gets fined a dollar toward the funds for Harry's House."

His announcement was greeted with catcalls and further teasing.

And then, finally, it was time to go. Because he was running late, he had to change and go to Marietta High School straight from the gym, so he didn't get the chance to see Stacey first.

He really hoped he wasn't going to let her down.

Jane McCullough caught him at the entrance to the school. "Tyler! I'm glad you're here. We were starting to worry."

"Hey, I wouldn't let you down," he reassured her. "I just got caught up at work."

She must have seen through the brittleness of his smile, though, because she put her hand on his arm. "Are you OK?"

"Yeah. I just don't want to make a prize idiot of myself," he admitted. "Everyone knows I can't cook."

"Remember what you're doing it for," she said. "That's more important—"

"—than my ego," he finished. "I know. And I want to do my best to help raise the money."

She patted his arm. "It's appreciated, believe me. Most of the bakers are in the teachers' lounge next to the kitchens."

Tyler peeked into the school cafeteria on the way. Eight of the folding tables were laid out as countertops with ingredients and equipment, and a name-card with each baker's name handwritten on them. Next to them was another table with four chairs, for the judges.

The other folding tables were lined in rows facing the bakers' tables, with chairs round them. From what he could see, the place was crowded; he knew the admission tickets were $10 each, so this would be a good start to the fundraising.

One side of the room had refreshment stalls offering tea, coffee, sodas, and cake—including the red velvet cupcakes Stacey had made. The other side had a mix of stalls set up by local businesses—everything from cosmetics and sweaters and shawls made from the wool from the local alpaca farm, through to jewelry made by Jillian at Tangled Charms and Sage Carrigan's amazing chocolates.

He was the second to last one to arrive in the teachers' lounge, and Jane handed him a black apron with Bachelor Bake-Off in big pink letters on the front. "Your uniform for the day."

"Seriously?" Tyler asked, pulling a face.

"It could be worse," Jake Price, the local public defender, said with a grin. "It's February now so everyone's thinking about Valentine's Day. They could've made us wear aprons covered in pink hearts."

Like Stacey's apron, Tyler thought. "Yeah."

"Or chef hats. Remember when Ry Henderson had to wear his posh Parisian chef's stuff for the Bachelor Auction in Grey's, the other year?" Avery Wainwright, the rodeo rider, asked.

"Do I," Tyler said wryly. "OK. I'll shut up and wear the apron."

He already knew Warren Hunt, the business manager at

the Graff Hotel, and Daniel Brer, a local portfolio manager who'd grown up in Marietta; and he'd just been introduced to finance whiz Zac Malone and wealthy financier Wes St. Claire when Jane McCullough came bustling through with her clipboard. "Everyone all set?" she asked.

"Sure," they chorused.

"Jodie Monroe—Harry's mom—is our MC. She's going to run through everything for the audience, introduce the judges, and explain what the prizes are," Jane said. "Good luck—and thanks for being good sports. I know some of you had your arms twisted and a couple of you were signed up without even being asked first."

"It's for a really good cause," Zac said.

"And those of us who can't cook—which is probably just me," Tyler said, "can live with the teasing."

"As you know, we're going to auction off the cookies in batches of a dozen afterward," Jane said.

Tyler had forgotten about that. If only he'd thought to give Stacey some money and ask her to buy his batches for him. Was it too late to text her and ask her?

He surreptitiously palmed his cell phone, only to discover there was no signal. Well, it was the middle of the high school, so of course there was some kind of signal blocker; they wouldn't want students being distracted by texts and what have you.

But it meant he was on his own.

"So good luck and may the best baker win!" Jane said

brightly.

A couple of minutes later, they were called through to set up their stations. Matthew West, the town veterinarian, arrived at the last minute and nodded to Tyler. Jodie introduced each of the bachelors in turn, then ran through the rules of the competition.

The ingredients were all set out on the table, along with a set of measuring spoons and cups, and to Tyler's relief so was the recipe. He'd done his best to memorize it but this was way out of his comfort zone—cooking in front of people when everyone knew he could practically burn water.

He scanned the crowd of people, looking for Stacey, and saw her sitting at a table with some other women he recognized as teachers and assistants at the elementary school. For her, he wanted to get this right.

She caught his eye and smiled at him, and suddenly everything felt good with the world. Until he looked at the judges. He knew Ryan Henderson, the pastry chef, and Sage Carrigan from the chocolate shop; Rachel Vaughn, the owner of Copper Mountain Gingerbread and Dessert Company, made up the trio of food specialists. They'd all know exactly what they were looking for from the bakers and would judge fairly but firmly on presentation, texture, and taste. The only wild card was Langdon Hale, the new fire chief; from what he'd heard, Langdon was quiet and a good judge of character. Tyler just hoped that Langdon might be less particular about cookies and would be the judge who gave good scores to be kind.

"Okay, bachelors, start your cookies!" Jodie rang a little bell, then stepped to the side.

Tyler dropped his box of eggs; to his horror, the whole lot broke, and he had to borrow a couple of eggs from Daniel, who was at the table next to his. But he managed to cream the butter and sugar without leaving lumps, added the eggs and vanilla and baking powder so it looked disgusting, then added the chocolate chips and the flour. Mud pies, he reminded himself, squishing the dough together.

Looking up from his table again once he'd put spoonfuls of dough on the cookie sheet was a mistake, because he could see his team from the gym. Sitting with them was Lyle Tate, looking hugely amused. Worse still, he saw Kelly get up from her table and go over to Stacey's table.

Oh, help.

He nearly dropped the first sheet full of dough, and had to force himself to concentrate on what he was doing. If he couldn't even get the dough into the stove, he might be the only baker in the group to get a first-round score of zero. Unless they'd take pity on him and give him a few marks for turning up and trying…

"Hi—you're Stacey, right?"

Stacey looked up to see a younger, dark-haired woman

standing next to her. "Y-yes."

"I'm Kelly—I work for Tyler," she said, holding her hand out. "It's good to meet you."

Stacey made herself take a deep breath so she wouldn't stutter. "Good to meet you, too, Kelly."

"So you're his secret weapon, then? Lyle Tate just told me you're teaching him to bake. Teaching Ty, that is, not Lyle," Kelly added with a smile.

Had Lyle also told her about the terms of their bet? Stacey wondered.

Clearly yes, because Kelly's brown eyes were sparkling. "You'd better hope Ty really doesn't come last, because Lyle Tate's kisses are mind-blowing."

"You're Lyle's g-girlfriend?" Stacey asked.

"Ex," Kelly said with a smile. "But we're still good friends."

"Uh-huh." Stacey could feel the other woman assessing her.

"I'm glad you're on our team," Kelly said, surprising her.

"Thank you."

"And you know they're auctioning off the cookies afterward? I was just thinking… Well, Ty dropped those eggs earlier." She bit her lip. "He really can't cook and I feel a bit guilty about signing him up for this, now. If he gets the temperature on the stove wrong or he doesn't set the timer properly…"

"I'm on it," Stacey said, understanding Kelly's worries

immediately. "Actually, I'd been thinking the same. I was going to bid whatever it takes to get them."

"There are going to be four lots of a dozen each. Say we buy two lots each?" Kelly asked.

"Done," Stacey promised. "I'll b-bid for the first two and you bid for the second two?"

"Done." Kelly winked at her. "Go, Team Carter."

"Team Carter," Stacey echoed.

Tara nudged her. "So you and Tyler are…?"

Stacey thought about denying it. But Carol Bingley had already started spreading gossip, and people might have seen her and Tyler out together in the town. She nodded shyly. "Though we started out as just friends. I remembered what you said."

"Maybe you're the one he's been waiting for," Tara said. "An awful lot of women will envy you."

"It's early days," Stacey said lightly. "Anything can happen." But she knew she'd already started to fall in love with Tyler. His earnestness, his passion, the way he wanted to change the world. She liked all that about him and more.

While the cookies were in the process of baking, Stacey went round the stalls with Tara. She bought one of the special Harry's House fundraiser bands from Jillian at Tangled Charms, which said "Harry's House" and had a silhouette of a house as well as a silhouette of a hammer and saw crossed over one another. She also bought some of Sage's dark salted caramels and a raffle ticket for a night in the honeymoon suite at the Graff Hotel; she was hardly going to use it herself if she won, but she thought it might be a nice treat for her aunt Joanie.

Finally, it was time for the judging. She could see all the bachelors looking awkward as the judges visited each table in turn, inspecting the cookies and cutting them open for a taste before going off to the side in a huddle to mark up their score sheets.

When they'd tasted the last batch, Langdon Hale, the new fire chief, came to the front to announce the scores.

"As judges we've been busy tasting the baked goods and scoring our bachelors on the appearance, taste, and texture of the cookies. All our bachelors have worked hard this afternoon, and I'd like you to put your hands together for them." He waited for the audience to applaud the bakers. "Thank you, everyone. The scores are, in reverse order: in eighth place, with choc chip cookies, Tyler Carter."

He'd come last.

Stacey was gutted for him, knowing how hard he'd worked. It took her attention away from the rest of the scores, until Langdon announced that the winner was the town veterinarian, Matthew West, with chocolate macadamia nut cookies. "And now I'll hand you back to Jodie," he finished, "to auction off the baked goods."

Stacey glanced over to Kelly, who gave her a thumbs-up to say she was ready.

Just as they'd planned, Stacey bought the first two lots of

Tyler's cookies, and Kelly bought the other two.

Lyle Tate strolled over to her table. "Good afternoon, ladies." He gave them a small bow. "Good to see the elementary school's finest out in force this afternoon."

"Oh, listen to you, Lyle," Tara said, laughing. "Don't tell me—Jane's asked you to come and charm everyone into buying an extra raffle ticket for the Graff's prize?"

"No, but if you'd like one I'd be happy to fetch it for you," he said with a grin. "Going to take me with you if you win, sugar?"

"Oh, be still, my beating heart," Tara teased, clutching both hands to her chest and laughing.

"It was worth a try. No, I'm here to claim my winnings." His blue eyes twinkled as he looked at Stacey. "Well, sugar, your man came last. So that's twenty dollars you owe me toward the Harry's House fund."

She took out her wallet and paid over the cash with a smile. "All for a good cause."

"And a kiss," he reminded her.

Even though Lyle was handsome, with his sandy hair and amazing blue eyes, the idea of kissing him felt more like kissing a brother. He didn't make her heart beat faster, the way Tyler did.

But she'd made the bet to kiss him if Tyler came last, and she wasn't going to renege. Though, when she pushed her chair back and stood up to kiss him, she was surprised when Lyle gallantly kissed her on the cheek.

"One kiss, paid in full," he said.

"But…" she began.

"Don't take me the wrong way, sugar. I would never force a girl to do anything she didn't want," he said softly. "I'm more likely to take down the kind of guy who does that sort of thing."

"I know. You just like flirting with all the girls in town."

"With so many beautiful women in Marietta, who could blame me?" he asked. "Out of interest, if you'd won, what song would you have made me sing?"

"Lady Gaga's 'Born This Way'," she said promptly.

He laughed. "Good choice. You're right about the flirting. It's how I am. But I'm still friends with every woman I've ever dated."

Kelly had said that she and Lyle were still friends, and something about the fireman made Stacey pretty sure he was just the same with his other exes. Maybe he was just searching for something he hadn't found yet. "That's good to hear." She paused. "Can I ask you something professionally?"

"About firefighting or ranching?" He looked surprised. "Sure, sugar. Go ahead."

Actually, she'd meant singing. "Do you know any songs about chickens?"

He blinked. "Chickens? I ranch cattle, sugar. I don't know much about—hang on, did you say songs?"

She nodded. "It's kind of an in-joke."

"With Carter? OK." He paused, clearly thinking about

it. "Well, off the top of my head, there's 'Dixie Chicken' by Garth Brooks, 'Little Red Rooster' by the Rolling Stones, and 'Do the Funky Chicken' by Rufus Thomas. Does that help?"

"It helps a lot." On impulse, she kissed his cheek. "Thank you."

"My pleasure, sugar." His smile faded slightly. "I'm glad Carter's picked a nice girl to date this time. The last one was beautiful, but she broke his heart. I don't think you'd do that."

"I'll try not to," she said. She didn't think Lyle was the type to gossip and she liked the fact that he was clearly looking out for Tyler. She had a feeling the men were good friends, despite the banter between them at FlintWorks.

"It's good to see you again, sugar," he said, and patted her on the shoulder. "Don't be a stranger."

Though, when Tyler walked over to join then, Lyle made the shape of an L on his forehead with his finger and his thumb. "What did you do wrong, Carter? Not pay enough attention to your teacher?"

Tyler rolled his eyes. "I left them in for about a minute too long, so the texture's…"

"… hard as a rock and burnt almost to the point where I'd need to get my firefighter gear," Lyle finished. "So I saw." He made another of the L-signs.

"Thanks, man," Tyler said dryly. "You wait till the next circuit class. You're going to hurt for *weeks* after."

"No, I'm not. You'll take pity on me because I'm the hero who saved the rest of the town from having to eat your cookies."

Tyler blinked. "You bid on them?"

"Two lots, actually—there's a stone wall I need to fix back at the ranch, and those cookies'll come in mighty handy," Lyle said with a grin.

"For those circuits," Tyler threatened, "I'm thinking single-leg burpee jumping jacks. Fifty on each leg and no swapping legs until the whole fifty's done."

"Bring it on," Lyle drawled, winked at Stacey, and went off to flirt with someone else.

"Just ignore what he said, Tyler," Tara said. "You did well up there. It's not easy having to do stuff with what feels like the whole world watching you."

"I still came last," Tyler pointed out.

"It's not the winning, it's the taking part," Mandy, one of the other teachers at the school, said.

He smiled. "Spoken like any good elementary school-teacher. Thanks, ladies, for trying to make me feel better."

"We meant it," Tara said. "I love baking, but it's a whole different ball game doing it in front of everyone in town. I would probably have dropped the eggs, too."

"Me, too," Mandy said.

Tyler looked at Stacey. "Don't say it."

"Thinking it," Stacey said with a smile, and lifted three fingers to her friends.

"We're going to head off, now," Tara said. "See you Monday, Stace. Catch you later, Tyler—if not before, then next Saturday, and we're going to cheer you on."

"Thanks for the support, ladies," Tyler said. "Next time you want to sit in the spa pool, it's on me. I'll make sure there's a note on the reception desk."

"Thank you. We'll take you up on that," Mandy said, and smiled at him.

Tyler took Stacey's hand when her friends had left them. "I'm sorry. I let you down. Everything you told me—I should've kept a closer eye on those cookies. I swear it was only a minute."

"You didn't let me down. Every stove's different," she said. "And you made money for Harry's House. That's the important thing."

"I know. But I am *so* not going to come last next week." Then he grimaced. "Actually, I probably am. We have to make pie. Uh." He grimaced again. "Pastry's meant to be harder than cookies. Ry Henderson spent years in Paris learning to do pastry. I don't stand a chance of learning it in a week."

"Yes, you do," Stacey said firmly. "You're not doing fancy French pastry. I can teach you basic pie crust, no problem."

"In a week, and considering I managed to mess up your failsafe cookies?"

She smiled. "It doesn't matter—you tried and that's the

important thing. People might tease you for a while, but you've done something positive to help Harry's House. Nobody can deny that."

"You have a point." He sighed. "So what did Kelly say?"

"We talked about being Team Carter," she said. "I think L-Lyle might've been yanking your chain about buying the cookies. Kelly and I arranged to buy the lots between us."

"I'll reimburse you both." He wrinkled his nose. "Sorry. I meant to ask you beforehand if you'd bid on them for me."

"No need. Anyway, it was Kelly's idea."

He nodded. "She's a good kid. She went a little bit wild after school, but then she came to work for me and it's all good now."

She'd already worked out that Lyle Tate was the kind of man who rescued people; it was beginning to sound as if Tyler was the same. "I think she feels a bit guilty about signing you up for the Bake-Off," Stacey said.

"I'll live," he said. "And I'm pretty sure she was egged on by quite a few others. I'm not going to blame her." He blew out a breath. "Right now I really need some recreation—something to take my mind off dropping eggs and messing up your failsafe recipe in front of half the town. Would you like to come ice-skating with me?"

Ice-skating? Panic flooded through her. "I can't s-skate."

"I'll teach you."

She trusted him, but this was *skating*—she'd always been hopeless at even walking on ice, let alone anything else. She'd fallen over all the time as a child, when it was icy; she still had the scars on her knees, and her mom had been so mad at how many clothes she'd ruined…

He stole a kiss. "Look at the boxing. You did way better than you thought you could at that, and this will be the same thing."

"Boxing's different," she said. "Then I'm on my feet on solid ground, not trying to b-balance on slippery ice on a t-tiny shred of metal."

"I promise I won't let you fall," he said softly, and she had a feeling he was talking about more than just the ice.

Plus she knew he was right about needing to let off steam. He'd faced a challenge and not done as well as he wanted, and now he needed to regain his balance—just as she did when she tackled things that didn't work out quite the way she planned them. She dealt with it by baking something complicated; he clearly needed something more physically challenging. "OK. Let's d-do it." She took a deep breath. "Do I need to change?"

"Your jeans are fine," he said, "but you might need a thicker sweater, plus a woolen hat and gloves, and you definitely need thick socks for skate boots."

"Can we go back to my apartment so I can change?"

"Sure we can," he said. "I'll pick up my skates while you're sorting out your sweater."

Since Tyler actually owned a pair of skates, Stacey thought, that meant he must feel very at home on the ice.

Then again, given what he did for a living, she wasn't surprised. She just hoped he didn't have any real expectations of her, or she'd disappoint him just as much as she'd always disappointed her father.

Once she'd changed into a thicker sweater, made sure she had a padded jacket and extra socks, he drove them to the parking lot by the courthouse.

"There's a rink in Marietta?" she asked surprised. She'd half expected him to drive them into the city.

"There's an outdoor rink at Miracle Lake," he said. "It freezes over, so everyone skates here December through March."

"It's so pretty," she said in delight. There were fairy lights strung through the trees, and the skate rental hut also sold hot chocolate. "I never knew this rink was here. I guess my friends aren't the—well—sporty type. Same as when I was a student in Bozeman."

"So what do you do to blow off steam?" he asked.

"Now or back then? Though I guess it's the same. The movies or the theater," she said. "Or cook something and put the world to rights over a bottle of wine."

"Sounds good. And the world would be a boring place if we all did exactly the same thing," he pointed out.

"I guess." Her father had always considered movies and the theater a waste of time, and she'd soon learned only to talk to her parents about what she was studying rather than what she did in her downtime.

"Let's go and sort out your skates."

It took Stacey a long while to get the hang of skating in a straight line, even with Tyler holding her hand. She knew her ineptness must be really frustrating for him, though to his credit he was patient with her and none of his frustration showed in his face. She really appreciated that; she'd spent too many years flinching inwardly and feeling stupid when she hadn't met her parents' expectations.

"You said you needed to blow off some steam," she said. "Why don't I sit out for a little while, so you can skate at your *real* skill level instead of letting me hold you back?"

He looked at her. "I asked you to come with me. I'm not going to just dump you in a corner and ignore you."

"Nobody puts Stacey in a corner," she deliberately misquoted. "And I'm happy to sit out for a bit and watch you. I'll be fine."

"Got it." He smiled at her. "Are you sure you don't mind?"

"Absolutely. It'll be fun to watch you," she said. "Go and show off."

"Yes, ma'am." He tipped his woolen hat at her, saw her safely to a bench at the side of the rink, then returned to the center.

Stacey watched him and was amazed at what he could do: skating backward, and doing complicated turns and spins. He was clearly enjoying himself, yet at the same time she noticed that he was careful with the people round him and made sure he didn't crowd anyone. Tyler Carter wasn't the kind to ride roughshod over others.

He skated back over to her bench. "Thank you. I needed that."

"No problem," she said brightly.

But some of her feelings of inadequacy must have shown in her face, because he kissed her. "Ice-skating isn't the easiest thing in the world, and you did great for a first time. I'm glad you came with me tonight. I wouldn't have wanted to share this with anyone else. Come for a last glide round the edge of the rink with me?"

Tyler Carter was one of life's nice guys. Was he just being kind, asking her to skate with him again when she was so hopeless?

Again, he seemed to guess at her thoughts. "I've blown off the crazies. There's nothing I want to do more right now than skate round the edge of the rink, hand in hand with my girl, then go to the rental hut for some hot chocolate and then kiss her until we're both dizzy."

She felt herself blush. "That's a plan."

He leaned forward and kissed her. "And then...something."

And she tingled all over.

With Tyler holding her hand, she managed to glide round the edge of the rink without falling over, and he helped her remove her skates before they headed to the rental hut for hot chocolate.

"You're really good at skating," she said.

"Thanks."

"Did you learn as a child?"

"No—not until I was a student. I used to play ice hockey," he said. "I loved it, but there's not much call for ice hockey in Marietta."

"Maybe you could set up a team?" she suggested.

"I think most of the guys in town prefer skiing or doing something on horseback." He smiled. "Anyway, if I missed hockey that much, I'd still be living in Bozeman where I could do it all the time."

"Bozeman's a beautiful city," she said. "Did you go to university there?"

"Yeah."

"Me, too." And she'd blossomed, away from her parents in Missoula.

"I like Bozeman well enough," he said, "but I'm happier back home, here in Marietta." He paused. "But I was thinking maybe we could go to Livingston tonight. Do you like Chinese food?"

"Love it," she said.

At the restaurant they chose egg rolls, noodles, a seafood dish of jumbo shrimp, scallops, and vegetables served on a sizzling platter, and moo shui pork with vegetables and pancakes.

"That has to be the most perfect Chinese meal ever," he said when they'd finished.

"Agreed," she said.

The waiter brought them the bill—which Stacey insisted on sharing—and a fortune cookie each.

"So what does yours say?" Tyler asked.

"Pick a path with heart," she said. It was something she'd done with her career; maybe it was time she did the same with her personal life.

He opened his. "Oh, dear. 'Be patient—in time even an egg will walk'." He gave her a rueful smile. "That, or it gets dropped in the middle of a Bake-Off in front of the whole town. I'm expecting omelet jokes from everyone at the gym for the next week."

She laughed. "Or you could say it's like your chicken thing and boxing. Lyle gave me some ideas for chicken songs, by the way."

"Uh-huh."

"Hey. It doesn't matter that you came last. At least you took part—you didn't chicken out," she said, squeezing his hand.

He groaned. "Enough with the chickens."

When he'd driven them back to their apartment block and they'd walked down to her front door, Stacey turned to him. "Would you like to come in for a glass of wine?" *Or something,* she added mentally.

"I'd like that," he said softly.

Chapter Eight

S TACEY HAD LEFT a table lamp on in her living room; rather than switch on the overhead lights, she switched on a second lamp and the room was suffused with soft light.

"Would you prefer red or white wine?" she asked.

"To be honest, right now I don't want wine," he said softly. "Instead, I'd really like to dance with you."

Her cheeks went pink. "Oh. OK. I, um… W-what sort of thing do you want to dance to?"

He knew from the stutter that he'd flustered her again. Which he hadn't meant to do: he just wanted to hold her. Dance with her. Kiss her. "May I?" he asked, gesturing to her speaker dock.

"S-sure."

He hooked up his phone and chose an old Lonestar favorite, "Amazed", then drew her into his arms.

It didn't matter that they were both dressed for ice-skating rather than dancing. It didn't matter that they were in her living room rather than in some nightclub. The only thing that mattered was that she was in his arms and he was holding her close.

They swayed together to the beat of the music, cheek to cheek; he couldn't resist turning his mouth very slightly so he could press the tiniest kiss against her cheek. Her skin was so, so soft, and she smelled of vanilla and strawberries.

The next thing he knew, her face turned very slightly to meet his, and at last his mouth skated against hers. The lightest, gentlest, sweetest touch that made every nerve end in his mouth tingle.

And then her head tipped back and she touched her lips to his in answer to his unspoken question: *yes.*

Need surged through him. He wanted to kiss her properly, feel her mouth open beneath his. He hadn't felt this kind of desire for a long, long time; part of him was scared, but he locked the emotions away in the back of his head. Not now. He wasn't going to let his past spill over and stop this. He needed this, and he had a feeling that Stacey needed it just as much.

She kissed him again, and it felt as if tiny stars were flickering in his head. When her mouth opened beneath his and the tip of her tongue touched his, the flickers became stronger and brighter. As if he was standing on top of the world and could see all the way to the edge of space, the brightness and the beauty and the crazy spirals.

"I want you," he whispered.

"I w-want you, too."

Was she stuttering because he was pushing her into

something she wasn't ready for, or was it because the emotion was overtaking her, too? Unsure, he pulled back slightly so he could look into her eyes. Tonight they were more blue than grey, and he really hoped he was reading this right.

"I think I've wanted you for a long, long time. Except I didn't know how much until tonight," he said.

She took a deep breath. "Me, too." And her face was filled with sincerity.

"Take me to bed, Stacey. Do with me what you will," he said.

In answer, she took his hand and led him through to her bedroom. She switched on the overhead light just long enough so she could turn on the light on her nightstand; and he wasn't surprised that the room was painted a soft duck-egg blue, with a white wrought-iron headboard on her queen-size bed and a traditional rug on the floor. Her bed linen was also duck-egg blue, embroidered with white daisies. And yet it felt relaxing and calming rather than over-fussy.

She bit her lip as she turned to him. "I, um… It's been a while for me."

"Me, too."

She took a deep breath. "I don't want to d-disappoint you, Tyler."

He wrapped his arms round her. "You're not going to disappoint me. Of course it's not going to be perfect, the first time. This is all about exploring. Finding out what each of us likes." He paused. "If I'm rushing you, I'll back off."

She shook her head. "You're not r-rushing me."

"Good." He stole a kiss. "I, um, bought a couple of condoms from the machine in the restroom at the Chinese restaurant. Not because I was expecting this, but just in case. Because I didn't think I had any, and if there are any tucked away then they're most likely out of date."

"Me, too." Her face went adorably pink. "For the s-same reason."

"Well, now. It'd be a shame to waste all that joint enterprise, wouldn't it?" he asked, and kissed her again.

His fingers slid under the hem of her sweater and up past the waistband of her jeans until he found bare skin. She shivered as he made tiny circles on her skin with his fingertips. And then, to his delight, he felt her palms splaying against his back. Skin to skin. Just what he'd really, really wanted.

She let him remove her thick sweater—and then he let her remove his.

Her thin T-shirt was next, followed by his.

She caught her breath. "I knew you'd look like…" She gestured to him, and blushed. "Well, y-you own a gym."

He smiled and stole a kiss. "I'm not vain, but thank you for the compliment." He traced the lacy outline of her bra with one finger. "And you're all curves. Beautiful." He could see in her expression that she was about to put herself down, and he kissed her lightly again. "Don't say it. You're lovely just the way you are. You're sweet and curvy, and I can't remember wanting anyone this much for a very long time."

He could see the moment that she relaxed again with him, and this time she let him undo the button and zip of her jeans, then slide the faded denim over her hips. He dropped to his knees and pressed a kiss just above her belly button. "You smell of vanilla."

"Shower gel," she said.

And cookies, he thought. It made him want to taste her.

Would she be shy with him again, hiding away from him, or could he make her self-control snap so she was her true self with him?

He finished helping her out of her jeans, removing her socks at the same time; and then she was standing in front of him wearing only a white lacy bra and matching knickers.

"So beautiful," he breathed.

"Y-you're wearing too much," she said.

He got to his feet. "I'm in your hands."

Almost shyly, she undid the button and zip of his jeans. He knew his reaction to her would be obvious through his soft cotton underpants, and the color in her face deepened as soon as she noticed.

But then she smiled and pulled the duvet back from the bed.

And, unable to resist, he picked her up and laid her back against the soft downy pillows.

"Well, now," he said as he knelt between her thighs.

"Just you and me." He dipped his head and nuzzled the hollow of her collarbones, then hooked one finger into the strap of her bra and drew it down. When he drew the other strap down, she tipped her head back and closed her eyes. And it was a moment's work to unclasp her bra and drop the lacy garment over the side of the bed.

"OK?" he asked softly.

She swallowed hard and nodded.

"If you want me to stop at any point, and I mean at any point," he said, "you tell me and I'll stop."

She opened her eyes and looked at him. "Even if...?"

He nodded, knowing exactly what she was asking. "Even if."

Had someone pushed her too far, too fast, in the past? he wondered. Not that he was going to ask her right now. He just wanted her to feel good about what they were doing.

"Thank you," she said softly, and cupped his cheek with one hand.

He turned his face to drop a kiss into her palm. "This is about you and me," he said. "About having fun." It had been a long time since he'd had fun in his personal life, and he was beginning to think it was the same for her.

He cupped her breasts in his hands, circling her nipples with his thumbs; again, she closed her eyes and tipped her head back, arching toward him and telling him with her body that she wanted more. He traced a path of kisses down from her collarbone; when he circled one nipple with the tip of his tongue, flicking against the hard peak, she gasped and pushed her fingers into his hair, urging him on.

Tyler loved the fact that she was so responsive to him. And he was thoroughly enjoying exploring her, finding out just where she liked to be touched and kissed, and how.

But what he really wanted was for her to explore him.

To take the lead and let herself go. To kiss him, touch him, stroke him, until they were both at fever pitch and desperate for the ultimate closeness.

"Stacey," he said softly. "Make love with me." He rolled over onto his back, bringing her with him so she was straddling him.

She gasped, looking shocked; but then understanding dawned in her expression and he knew she'd worked out his intentions. He was letting her take the lead.

Then she dipped her head, caught his lower lip between hers, and nipped gently until he opened his mouth and let her deepen the kiss.

Tyler loved every second of this. The way her fingertips skated over his skin made him quiver, and the feel of her mouth against his throat made him reach up to grip her headboard and try to keep his control. He wanted to take this slowly and wring every ounce of pleasure from it—for both of them. And so he let her explore him, let her touch him how and where she wanted. He dragged in a breath as her fingers dipped under the hem of his underpants, and he felt her draw the soft material downward. He couldn't help closing his eyes as she touched him, sliding her fingers round his shaft. She made him ache; and right at that moment he wanted to be inside her. The ultimate closeness.

"Stacey," he whispered. "I want you so badly, it hurts."

"Me, too," she whispered back.

"The condoms are in the back pocket of my jeans," he said.

"OK."

He felt the mattress shift as she climbed off the bed and found the packet in his jeans.

"Now?" she asked, returning to the bed.

"Now," he confirmed, and a tremor ran through him as she undid the little foil packet and smoothed the condom over his shaft.

"Make love with me," she said, and lay down next to him.

He didn't need a second invitation; and then it was exactly what he'd been thinking about all week, with Stacey leaning back against her pillows, her hair slightly mussed and her mouth parted and those beautiful blue-grey eyed filled with desire. He knelt between her thighs and dipped his head to kiss her as he eased into her.

"OK?" he asked.

"Very OK," she confirmed.

And then he pushed deeper, watching her eyes widen with pleasure and feeling her breasts tightening against his check. He could hear her making little breathy sighs and tiny, incoherent murmurs, and he was aware of the pleasure spiraling through his own body.

"Let go," he whispered. "Because I'll catch you."

He felt her body start to ripple round him, and he wrapped his arms tightly round her, holding her close as they both fell over the edge into their climax.

When their breathing had slowed to normal, he gently withdrew.

"Can I use your bathroom?" he asked.

"Sure. It's the door over there," she said, gesturing toward her en suite.

Once he'd dealt with the condom, he grimaced. What now? He hadn't thought to grab any of his clothes from the floor; and he was pretty sure that Stacey would have gone shy on him. Would she want him to dress and leave? Or would she want him to stay?

He had no idea. So he was going to have to bite the bullet and ask her.

He walked back into her bedroom, and she'd pulled the duvet over herself.

"Sorry. I didn't think to…" He gestured to the pile of clothing on the floor. "Maybe you should close your eyes?"

He'd kind of hoped that it would make her laugh and tell him not to be so ridiculous; considering the intimacy they'd just shared, there was no need for her to be shy with him.

But when she said nothing, he risked a glance and realized that she had actually closed her eyes.

OK.

He pulled on his underpants, then went to sit on the bed. "Stacey."

She opened her eyes again. "So what happens now?" she asked.

"I don't know," he said honestly. "Do you want me to go? Or do you want me to stay?"

"I don't do this kind of thing very often," she said. "Hardly ever. I have no idea what the etiquette is."

"It's negotiable," he said. "Do you want me to stay or go?"

"Honestly?"

"Honestly."

"Both," she admitted. "I feel kind of awkward. But, at the same time..." She let the words trail off.

"Me, too," he said. "We're new at this. At least, you and me together," he amended.

"So do you want to stay or go?" she asked.

"Both," he said. "But just a tiny bit more of me wants to climb back in that bed with you, hold you, and go to sleep with you in my arms."

"I'd like that, too. But..." She bit her lip.

"We're still working out how this thing works between us," he said. "What just happened...that's between you and me. I wasn't even planning on dating anyone, let alone anything else—my focus has been totally on my business.

This came out of the blue. So if I'm totally honest with you, right now I can't say whether this is for now or for always, and I'm guessing it's the same for you."

She nodded.

"So maybe," he said, "we should both stop overthinking it and just let it happen, see where it goes."

"Sounds good to me." She looked at him. "So are you planning on sitting there for the rest of the evening, or are you getting back under the covers?"

He smiled. "I'm taking that as an invitation." He climbed back under the duvet and drew her into his arms. "I'm working the late shift tomorrow, so I won't wake you three hours before the crack of dawn."

She blinked. "People really go to the gym that early?"

"We open slightly later on a Sunday," he said. "But yes, we have people who like to do their workout first thing before work on a weekday because it sets them up for the day."

"Well, if you're not working first thing tomorrow, maybe we could do that pastry lesson," she suggested. "Meaning you make us breakfast."

"Pastry for breakfast?" he asked, mystified.

"Pie."

"Ah. As a personal trainer, I really ought to protest about healthy eating," he said with a grin.

"Pie with cream," she added. "Or ice cream. Or both."

His grin broadened as he realized she was teasing. "Make

that really, *really* protest," he teased right back.

"Joking apart, Sunday morning means pancakes, right? Pie isn't so different. Anyway, I don't eat pie for breakfast every day," she said.

"So what do you eat for breakfast?" he asked, curious.

"Oatmeal. Made with flax seed and blueberries, and no sugar."

So she ate healthily. Actually, he wasn't so surprised. He'd already worked out that she liked baking, but what she liked more was baking for other people to enjoy.

"In fact," she said thoughtfully, "you could say that tomorrow morning I was just planning on swapping the porridge for pastry."

"And cream," he reminded her.

She gave him the cutest, cutest grin. "Yeah. And cream." She paused. "Actually, I should've asked instead of assuming. Do you actually like blueberry pie?"

"It's my favorite," he said, "and, speaking on a professional level, blueberries are a superfood—so it's not as bad as eating one of those pies full of toffee and cream and marshmallows."

"Then we'll make blueberry pie tomorrow," she said.

It felt weirdly domestic, and very different from the life he'd shared with Janine. She'd worked long hours and hadn't been that keen on cooking, either, so they'd always eaten out on the way home from work or bought takeout; whereas Stacey actually enjoyed cooking and was perfectly at home in the kitchen.

"Blueberry pie," he agreed.

She lay curled in his arms; Tyler heard her breathing become slower and deeper as she fell asleep, but he was still wide awake—and brooding, thinking of the last time he'd shared a bed with someone.

He and Janine had ended up sleeping with their backs to each other. They hadn't been able to take comfort in each other; after the miscarriage, he hadn't had the right words and neither had she. Even during the night, they hadn't ended up curling into each other's arms—and the gap between them had just got bigger and bigger. The more time went on, the more it seemed impossible to bridge it.

He'd thrown himself more and more into work, not delegating a single thing—even though he trusted his team to run things just as well as he did. It was simply easier to tire himself out physically than to face Janine and know that he could never, ever make up for what she'd been through. Nothing he could say would make things better. Nothing he could do would make things better. Nothing he *was* would make things better.

It was hardly surprising that Janine had gone back to her mother in Bozeman, and he'd left it too long before trying to win her back. He'd learned from his mistakes—not communicating was the quickest way to kill a relationship—but, at the same time, this whole thing with Stacey scared him stupid. He needed to move on, and he was pretty sure she was the one he wanted to move on with. But supposing he got it wrong again? It was a huge, huge risk. Had he done the right thing by taking it?

THE NEXT MORNING, Stacey woke in Tyler's arms. He was still asleep; not wanting to wake him, she lay there quietly. She couldn't even remember the last time she'd woken up in someone's arms; after her last relationship had crashed and burned, she'd given up on the idea of being with someone and concentrated on her career.

She didn't think Tyler would be like her exes and be scared off by her father. But was this thing between them going too far, too fast? Was she just setting herself up for failure again? Would she disappoint him? The doubts spun round and round in her head.

She'd just about worked out how to say to Tyler that last night had been amazing but she thought they'd be better off being just good friends, when he opened his eyes.

"Good morning," he said.

"Um, good m-morning," she replied, all flustered because the words had just gone out of her head again.

He kissed her. "It's a good morning, because I've woken up with you," he said softly.

The heat in his eyes sent answering heat through her, and her nagging doubts were forgotten when he made love with her again, then soaped her thoroughly in the shower afterward and dried her tenderly with a towel.

"So, Madam Teacher," he said. "I need some clean clothes—how about I go next door, get changed and make us both a decent cup of coffee, and then we have our baking lesson?"

"Sounds good to me," she said.

And she was still smiling by the time she'd set out all the ingredients for the pie and he'd come back in bearing an espresso for himself and a cappuccino for her. "A spoonful of sugar, right?" he asked with a smile.

"Perfect. Thank you." She smiled back. "Ready to start making pastry?"

"Ready," he confirmed.

"OK. I've already turned the stove on to preheat it. The two things you need to know about pastry: first, keep the handling to a minimum, and second, don't add too much water or the pastry will go hard."

"Minimum handling, and easy on the water." He frowned. "Why minimum handling?"

"Because you're trying to minimize the formation of gluten. The idea is that the fat coats the flour cells and makes it hard for the water to hydrate the flour, so the pastry goes all nice and flaky," she explained.

"OK. So what do I do?"

"Two cups of all-purpose flour into the big bowl," she said.

He measured them out.

"A stick of butter—straight from the fridge, then cut into small dice so it's quicker for you to rub in and the fat stays as cold as possible."

"Rub in?"

"Cut up the butter, and then I'll show you," she said.

He started to dice the butter. "Is this small enough?"

"A little bit smaller," she said.

He cut the rest of it up into smaller pieces.

"OK. Rubbing in."

"Tip the butter into the flour," she said.

When he'd done so, she demonstrated rubbing in. "Rub small amounts between your fingers and your thumbs, like this, and keep your hands out of the bowl so you keep the mixture as cool as possible. You want it to look like bread-crumbs."

He moved to stand behind her, then put his hands into the bowl so she was held close against his body. "Like this."

"Uh-huh." Stacey was aware how croaky her voice sounded.

He pressed a kiss against the curve of her neck. "Keep it cool, hmm?"

She knew he meant the pastry and he was teasing her, but all the same a shiver of desire ran through her.

"You're supposed to p-pay attention to the teacher."

"Yes, Miss Allman." This time, he nibbled her earlobe.

"And d-distracting your teacher," she said, "is the quickest way to guarantee your pastry will be hard."

He chuckled. "Pastry. Now there's a good word for it."

She felt herself flush to the roots of her hair. Her double entendre had been totally unintentional. "Um."

He spun her round and stole a kiss. "Sorry. That's unfair of me, especially as you're giving up your time to help me. I'll behave. Tell me when it looks like breadcrumbs."

"You're telling me you don't know what breadcrumbs look like?"

"I don't cook. At all," he reminded her. "I'm the one whose grilled cheese set off the smoke alarm in the staff kitchen and the fire crew heard it from the other side of the road. And remember you offered to help me after I set off the smoke alarm here, too?"

"Point taken. Keep going," she said.

Finally, the pastry was at the stage where he could add the salt. "And now two or three tablespoons of cold water. Less is better. You can always add more but you can't take it away," she said.

He added two tablespoons of water. "What happens if I add too much?" he asked.

Clearly he was worried that it might happen on the day by accident. "You can add more flour, and you might have to knead the pastry a bit more on the pastry board to work the flour in," she said.

"Right."

"Mix it with a knife and the crumbs will start to come

together to make the dough," she said.

He followed her instructions until he had a ball of sticky dough; then she showed him how to knead the dough lightly.

"And then you put the pastry in plastic wrap in the fridge so it can rest."

"Why?" he asked.

"It makes the pastry easier to work with and means it holds its shape better," she said. "It gives the water a chance to diffuse through the dough and relax the gluten strands."

He smiled at her. "My gorgeous science girl."

"If you understand why something works, you remember the method better," she said.

He kissed her. "You're a secret nerd, aren't you?"

"Not so secret," she said ruefully.

"I like it," he said. "OK. So what do we do while the pastry rests?"

"Grease the pie plate and make the filling," she said promptly.

Once he'd followed her instructions to grease the pie plate and put blueberries in a bowl with sugar and flour, ready to go in the pie, it was time to roll out the pastry.

"The base needs to be bigger than the lid," she said, "so you divide the dough into not quite equal halves, and roll each part into a ball so you can roll it into a circle. You dust the marble board and the rolling pin with flour, so the pastry doesn't stick to it—and then you roll the pastry with even strokes away from you, giving the dough a quarter turn between each roll." She demonstrated the first couple of turns and then let him take over.

The pastry wasn't even, and by the time he'd finished the circle shape she'd started was totally lopsided.

"Help?" he asked.

"Roll it back into a ball and put it back in the fridge for five minutes to cool down," she said, "while we make the lid."

This time, he rolled the pastry evenly. "I've actually got a circle."

She kissed him. "Don't sound so surprised."

"This is way harder than ice-skating," he said. "I can turn a perfect circle there. But give me a rolling pin…"

"Believe in yourself," she said. "You've got this." She retrieved the dough from the fridge.

This time, the dough was more or less in a circle.

"I take it there's an easy way to get it into the pie plate?" he asked.

"You fold it into quarters," she said, showing him how, "then put it in the pie plate and unfold it. Press the pastry into the bottom and the sides so it's even."

"So far, so good," he said when he'd done it.

"Add the filling—and dot a little bit of butter on top," she said.

"And now I put the lid on?"

"You brush the edges with water first so it's easier to seal the pastry," she said, handing him a pastry brush.

He followed her instructions.

"Trim off the excess." She demonstrated the first half.

His half was a bit less even, but he guessed it was reasonable for a first effort. He'd practice so it looked better by Saturday's Bake-Off.

"Then you seal the pastry—just press a fork around the edge." Again, she showed him the first half and let him do the second half.

"Then cut a couple of slits in the top so the steam can escape, and put it in the stove at 425 for about half an hour—the pastry will be golden and the blueberry juice will just start to bubble through the slits." She handed him the oven gloves. "Remember how to set the timer?"

He nodded.

"It's all yours," she said with a smile.

Once he'd put the pie in to cook, he drew her over to the little bistro table in the corner of her kitchen and scooped her onto his lap. "So you'll write down your blueberry pie recipe for me?"

"If you like it," she said. "Or we could do something else, if you'd rather."

"Blueberry pie's good for me," he said. "Nice and simple." He kissed her. "I'm going to write the first draft of my proposal for the kids' exercise classes today—Sundays are fairly quiet so I can catch up with my admin at the gym. Would you mind looking it over when I'm done, to see if

I've missed anything or got anything way off beam?"

"Sure," she said. "I'd be glad to."

"Thank you." He kissed her again. "I like working with you."

"It's hardly working—I just made a couple of suggestions. Most of it was you."

"But the baking has been mainly you. You've been brilliant. So don't put yourself down." He paused. "And I'm betting I'm not the only one who says that."

"My aunt Joanie says the same," she admitted.

"So why can't you see how great you are, Stacey?" he asked.

"I'm just ordinary," she said, squirming. "And people who boast about themselves when they're nothing special—well, everyone laughs at them."

"Would I be guessing right if I said that was something your dad used to say?"

She looked away. "Do we have to t-talk about this?"

"No. But would you let your kids be defined by one person's opinion?" he asked.

"Of course not."

"Then it applies to you, too," he said softly.

"So have you thought about what kind of cake you want to make?" she asked brightly, desperate to change the subject.

To her relief, he didn't call her on it. But he didn't let go of her, either. He kept holding her close, almost cherishing her. "Given the mess I made of it last time, probably not a layer cake," he said. "What would you recommend?"

"Maybe a glazed cake," she said. "Because then you only have one cake pan to think about and you don't have to worry about two layers being even."

"Glazed cake sounds good."

And then the timer on the stove pinged, saving her from the risk of any more awkward conversation.

The pie looked perfect. She made them both a mug of coffee to go with it, set the table, and put a jug of cream next to the pie and the pie-server.

"Ready for this?" she asked.

"Ready." He took a deep breath, and cut a slice of pie for her and another for himself. "Does it look OK?"

"I can't see any sogginess," she said. "But you know what they say about the proof of the pudding…"

He poured cream on top, then took a mouthful. "Oh. It actually tastes all right."

"It's good," she said, when she tried a mouthful. "You ought to take the rest of the pie with you this morning to share with your team at the gym."

"Are you sure?" he asked.

"Absolutely."

When they'd finished breakfast and cleared up, he kissed her again. "I need to get going. But thank you for the lesson."

"My pleasure." She smiled at him. "And I'll write down this recipe for you so you can practice."

"I'm going to be late tonight, but see you tomorrow, maybe?"

"I'm going over to Tara's with some of our other colleagues tomorrow," she said. "We're having a movie night. How about Tuesday?"

"Tuesday's good. I'll cook—well, order in the main course from Rocco's, and we'll have pie and ice cream for dessert," he said.

She smiled. "I'll email you the recipe, then."

"Thanks." He kissed her again. "Tuesday. Seven."

"I'll be there."

Chapter Nine

"SHE'S A KEEPER," Kelly said after her first taste of the blueberry pie. "If she can teach you to do this... Yeah. Stacey's a keeper."

"She's my friend," Tyler said.

"I don't think so. Friends don't put the smile back in your eyes like that," Kelly said.

He sighed. "It's early days. I'm not making any promises to anyone. And Stacey would really, really hate it if she knew people were gossiping about her."

"I'm not gossiping. I'm talking to you," Kelly said. "Is there cream with this?"

"No. Think yourself lucky you get pie at all."

"Hey. I deserve pie. I bought half your cookies yesterday to save your ass," Kelly reminded him. "*And* I cleaned the bathrooms this morning."

"Because you're on the roster to do the ladies', and I cleaned the men's room," Tyler said. "And I'll reimburse you for the cookies."

She shook her head. "I feel the tiniest bit guilty about

158

signing you up. Then again, if I hadn't, you wouldn't have met Stacey."

"I live next door to her," Tyler pointed out.

"Yeah, but you've lived next door to her for..." She flapped a dismissive hand. "Well, however long. Without the Bachelor Bake-Off, you wouldn't have got to know her better, would you? You'd still have been at nods and smiles in the lobby."

"So you've done me this huge favor and you deserve a pay rise, right?"

Kelly grinned. "I'm not pushing my luck that far. Seriously, Ty, it's good to see you looking... Well, *happy*. Even if you do look a bit goofy."

He rolled his eyes. "I do not look goofy."

"Yeah, you do." She patted his shoulder. "And that's good, too."

"Hmm. So is the pie OK?"

"For a first attempt, ten out of ten. But you've got a pastry chef judging you on Saturday. You need to even up the edging a bit," Kelly said.

"See, this is what I like about you. You tell me things straight."

"Most bosses don't want to hear things straight," Kelly said. "And most bosses delegate the bathroom cleaning instead of doing their fair share. You're different."

"Thank you for the compliment."

"It's just a fact." She paused. "Can I have more pie?"

"Knock yourself out," Tyler said, gesturing to the pie plate. "I'm going to work on this proposal for classes. Give me a yell if you need anything."

"More pie," she said, helping herself to a second slice. "And I will."

He grinned, and got on with writing up his proposal. And it was a good excuse to email Stacey. Just to say hi.

She emailed him back with the pie recipe and a smiley face.

And maybe Kelly had a point. Maybe he was different. He certainly felt lighter of heart since he'd started seeing Stacey. Maybe, just maybe, this was going to work out.

HE TEXTED HER on Monday to ask what she'd like him to order from Rocco's.

I love all Italian food. Choose your favorite, she texted back.

That was an easy one. Cannelloni, garlic dough balls, and a crisp salad. And that, he thought, would go very nicely with the blueberry pie.

ON TUESDAY AFTERNOON, Tyler made pastry.

Or, to be accurate, he made two lots of pastry. The first

batch, he accidentally added too much water and it was such a mess that he couldn't get it to feel like smooth dough, no matter how much flour he added. The second batch felt as if it was maybe a little too dry, but after the disaster of the first batch he didn't dare add any more water. He just rolled it out, and when it cracked a bit as he unfolded the base into the pie plate he patched it up with some leftover pastry and hoped that would be enough.

There were a few blueberries left in the box when he'd measured out six cups; it seemed a shame to waste them, so he added them in before placing the pie lid on the top. Remembering Kelly's comment about presentation, he made more effort to make the fork marks round the edge more even. But it was hard when the pastry was so crumbly.

He put the uncooked pie in the fridge, ready to put it in the stove as soon as the food from Rocco's arrived, and had just about cleared up all the flour by the time Stacey rang the doorbell.

She smiled. "I can see the pastry practice went well."

"How?"

She ruffled his hair. "Flour. Right here."

He groaned. "Sorry. I was busy cleaning up the kitchen."

She kissed him lightly. "You look fine. I brought you this as my contribution to dinner." She handed him a tub of seriously good vanilla ice cream and a bottle of red wine. "I'm assuming this goes OK?"

"It does indeed. Thank you." He kissed her back.

Ten minutes later, his order arrived from Rocco's.

"Great choice. I love cannelloni," she said. "What can I do to help?"

"Just sit there," he said, gesturing to his dining table, and served up.

He put the pie in the oven, mentally crossing his fingers, and set the timer for thirty minutes.

"This is lovely," she said.

"Because I didn't cook it," he said with a grin. "I'm assuming you know how to make this stuff?"

"It's not as complicated as you think. You can get ready-to-bake cannelloni tubes—all you need to do is make the ragù and the béchamel sauce, fill the tubes with the ragù and cover them with béchamel, grate a little cheese over the top, and bake it."

"In my case, that'd be burn it," he said, wrinkling his nose.

"Give it a try," she said.

With her by his side, he could be tempted.

"How was the movie last night?" he asked.

She smiled. "A *Pride and Prejudice* marathon. The Colin Firth version."

"You don't need to say any more," he said. "That's my sister's favorite series of all time."

"Your sister has good taste." She raised her eyebrows. "Not your thing, I'm guessing?"

"Not my thing," he said. "Can you imagine how awful it

was to live in Regency England? All that snobbery—and people didn't even dress themselves."

"Rich people didn't dress themselves," she corrected. "But I hear you on the snobbery. And women were so limited in what they could do." She raised an eyebrow. "It's still a good series though."

"Because it has the bit with Colin Firth swimming in it and getting out of the pond in wet clothes?"

She laughed. "Not just because of that." She paused. "I've been through your draft proposal, by the way. I printed it out and made a couple of suggestions. But basically it's really good and I'm sure both the school and Harry's House will beg you to do it."

"Thank you."

And then he was horribly aware of the smell of something burning.

Oh, no.

"Excuse me a second," he said, and rushed over to the stove.

When he opened the door, he could see exactly what had happened. The pastry casing had split in the wrong places and the filling had oozed through. Just like the cake batter, the filling had fallen onto the floor of the stove, and was happily burning. Great.

"Is everything OK?" she called.

He wasn't going to try to lie his way through it. Not when she could smell the problem for herself. "Bit of a pie filling crisis," he said, taking the pie out of the stove and resting it on the top. "I had some leftover blueberries so I put them in as well. I probably should've left them." He sighed. "At least the pastry looks done. But it's split in the wrong places."

She came over. "You didn't use quite enough water so it's gone very short and brittle on you."

He grimaced. "That was attempt number two. I put too much water in, the first time, and it just stayed sticky no matter how much flour I put in, so I gave up on that batch and tried again."

"And then you overcompensated for overdoing the water, the first time round," she said. "But the only way you learn how to do something is to try doing it. It's OK to get things wrong."

Exactly what he told his clients if they found it hard to do a particular movement. But when you were the getting it wrong, it felt bad. "As long as it doesn't go wrong on Saturday. I know the most important thing is raising money for Harry's House, but it'd be nice not to come last again."

"You'll be fine," she said with a smile.

He looked at the offending pie. "It looks a mess. Are you sure you want to eat it?"

"Yes."

And even if it was utterly disgusting, he was sure that she'd eat it. Just to make him feel better about himself. Stacey Allman was one of the nicest women he'd ever met.

"Here goes," he said, and cut a slice of pie.

The pastry was hideously crumbly, and it fell apart between the pie plate and the dessert dish. He'd give himself zero points for presentation. His thoughts must've shown on his face, because Stacey kissed him. "Today it's not what it looks like, it's what it tastes like. You just need to put some ice cream on the top to hide the broken pie crust, and it all tastes the same. It's *fine.*"

Yeah. She was definitely one of the nicest women he'd ever met.

And he really ought to tell her about Janine. Be honest with her about who he really was.

But he needed to find the right words.

He served up a second slice of pie, which was equally as crumbly and messy as the first, and added ice cream to both bowls.

"It's lovely," she said after the first spoonful.

He tasted it, too. "It's not the best pie I've ever eaten."

"And it's not the worst. It's only the second time you've ever made pie, and the first time you made it on your own," she pointed out. "You've done well. Really. I wouldn't lie to you."

"But you'd eat it even if you hated it, so as not to hurt my feelings," he said.

She wrinkled her nose. "Let's just say I choose my battles carefully. And no, I don't like hurting people's feelings. What does it achieve, making someone feel bad? Unless," she added thoughtfully, "it's the only way you can make yourself feel in control of things."

"That sounds personal."

"Some of my students," she said.

Or maybe her father.

But he wasn't going to push her about that.

"I had an email from Jane McCullough today about Saturday," he said. "Apparently we're doing a Chinese auction at the Bake-Off."

"What's a Chinese auction?" she asked.

He reached over and squeezed her hand. "I'm glad I'm not the only one who didn't know what it was. I asked Jane, and she said the lots for the auction are all on a table with a basket in front of each one. You buy strips of raffle tickets and place your tickets in the basket matching the prize you want to win—it's up to you how many tickets you put in each basket, and you can put your tickets in however many baskets you want. The winning ticket is drawn from each basket at the end of the evening."

"So you need prizes?" she asked. "I can buy a couple of things to donate."

"Apparently," he said, "the auction prizes are the bachelors."

She blinked. "She's auctioning *you* off?"

"No, that came out wrong—she's auctioning the baskets. The bachelors provide the basket—and it's meant to represent what I love about Marietta." He frowned. "The only thing is, the things I love about Marietta can't be bought. The sense of community. The way everyone looks out for everyone else. The fresh air. Being able to walk for miles. Huge skies."

"Mm, I see what you mean—that's tricky to represent, unless you buy a painting or something." She looked at him. "But you can sell you."

He blinked. "Me?"

"Carter's Gym," she said. "Maybe offer things that you love most about your work."

"So a couple of personal training sessions, a voucher for a sauna and pool session, and maybe a six-week course of exercise classes," he said. "That would work." He smiled. "And now I've been introduced to them, some of Sage Carrigan's amazing chocolates. And a voucher for dinner for two and a bottle of wine at FlintWorks."

"If you sort the vouchers and the chocolates," she said, "I can help you make up the basket with cellophane and ribbons and what have you."

"Thanks—that'd be really good."

She helped him wash up, and then he put the radio on and they curled up together on his sofa.

"So can I try cooking pie for you again on Thursday?" he asked.

"That'd be good."

"Great. I'm being interviewed on Marietta Radio on Thursday afternoon, on Lacey Hathaway's drive time show," he told her.

"That's broadcast between three and six, isn't it?" she asked. "I listen sometimes on the way home from school."

"So maybe I could do the pie after that?"

"Why don't I cook the main course?" she suggested. "You could bring the uncooked pie with you and we can cook it in my stove. What time's your interview?"

"Four."

"So we could eat at seven."

"Sounds good to me." He paused. "And maybe we can do another boxing session, this week."

"I'd like that. Maybe at the weekend?" she asked.

"The weekend's good. I'll need to check my schedule for the roster," he said.

And funny how making plans with her felt good. He'd avoided that kind of thing for so long.

But he really, really needed to tell her about Janine.

ON THURSDAY, STACEY had cooked baked potatoes, baked chicken with a spice rub, and steamed baby broccoli and baby carrots. "I thought I'd keep it simple," she said.

And healthy, he thought. "It's wonderful. Thank you."

"I heard you on the radio this afternoon. You sounded good," she said. "So making pastry's really harder than doing an hour of high intensity interval training?"

"I meant every word I said," he told her feelingly.

She grinned. "I bet lots of your clients are going to turn up with baked goods over the next week."

"If they do, then I can invite everyone to help themselves to the goodies, in return for a donation to Harry's House," he said with a grin. "Including my team. Who appreciated the last two pies, by the way."

"See? I told you it wasn't that bad. This one won't be, either."

Her faith in him seemed substantiated, because this time his pie filling didn't spill over or burn. It looked suspiciously good. It didn't fall apart when he cut it. And, to Tyler's surprise, it actually tasted OK, too.

"I think you'll be fine for Saturday," Stacey said. "This is great."

"Uh-huh."

"Are you OK?" she asked, a tiny frown pleating her forehead. "You seem a bit distracted."

Because he was. And he couldn't put this off anymore. It wasn't fair to her. "Stacey, we need to talk."

"Ah." For a second, hurt flashed across her face, and then she gave him the brightest, brightest smile.

She obviously thought he was breaking up with her.

And it had clearly happened like that for her before.

Except, when he'd finished telling her what was in his heart, she might be the one doing the breaking up. It was a risk he'd have to take if he was to stand any chance of moving on.

"It's not about us. It's about the fact I'm not the man you think I am. It's about what happened with my ex, Janine," he said. "Nobody else in Marietta knows the full story—not even my family—but since you and are…" Involved, but he wasn't sure how to put it. "Anyway, I think I owe it to you to tell you the truth."

"It won't go any further than me. I don't gossip," she said.

He already knew that without having to ask, but it was good to have it confirmed. "Thank you." He took a deep breath. "I met Janine about five years ago in Bozeman, at a party thrown by a mutual friend. She worked in hotel management and I was the manager of a gym. We just clicked. We took it slowly, but I was pretty sure she was the love of my life and I knew we were going to settle down together."

Stacey said nothing, and he continued. "I knew I didn't want to live in Bozeman forever; I wanted to come home to Marietta. Then I had the opportunity to buy the gym here, and it seemed like perfect timing. I persuaded her to come back here with me so I could open the business—except she never really settled here."

He grimaced. "She'd always lived in a city, and she hated life in a small town. She really didn't like the way everyone knew everything about you. I thought she'd grow to like it here, because Marietta's such a special place, but now I realize I was being selfish and expecting her to change to suit me."

He looked away. "Maybe we could've muddled through. But then she fell pregnant. We hadn't planned it—I was still building up the business and she was commuting every day to Bozeman. She didn't want me to tell anyone about the baby until she was twelve weeks' pregnant, and she wanted to see her doctor back in Bozeman rather than the doctors here. I agreed, because I thought maybe this was our chance to make a real go of things. I loved the idea of being a dad and bringing up my child in the place where I grew up. Teaching my child to swim in the river where I learned to swim. And I thought maybe she could work with me in the gym, or maybe she could find a job locally, so she wouldn't have to commute. That we'd be a real family…" He swallowed hard. "But then she had a miscarriage at ten weeks."

Stacey reached over to squeeze his hand. "I'm so sorry."

"Things between us got worse after that. I was grieving, too, so I threw myself into the business so I didn't have time to think about what was happening—and the gulf between us got wider and wider. I should've thought of her needs instead of being selfish. She hated it in Marietta. So she went back to her mom's in Bozeman for a while. I should've gone after her straight away—but I thought maybe some time apart would do us both good."

And how very wrong he'd been.

"I kept making excuses that I was busy at work, instead

of facing how unhappy she was—because I knew there was nothing I could do to make things right for her. For us. When I finally went to see her, she told me she wasn't coming back and she'd been offered a dream job as the manager of a big hotel in Billings." He bit his lip. "I really didn't want to live in Billings, but if that's what it would've taken to make her happy, I would've sold the gym here and gone with her. But she didn't ask me to go with her. I didn't feel I was enough for her. And so I let her leave."

AND JANINE HAD clearly taken his heart with her.

"I'm sorry it worked out that way for you," she said gently. "And I know the feeling about not being enough for someone. But it's really not true of you, Tyler. Everyone in Marietta loves you." She paused. "You did get one thing wrong, though."

He frowned. "What?"

"You're exactly who I think you are. You're a good man, who cares about others—and who's only human, just like the rest of us. Everyone makes mistakes."

"I let Janine down. Really badly."

"It takes two to break a relationship," she said. "What happened to you both was really sad, and it's not surprising that you were both hurting too badly to talk things through. Sometimes things hurt too much to talk about. But you can't take all the blame for it."

"I don't think I'll ever stop feeling guilty," he admitted.

"It wasn't your fault that Janine lost the baby—or her fault," Stacey said. "And yes, you both could've handled things differently. But that's really easy to say in hindsight, and I think anyone in that situation would struggle to deal with it." And now she knew the truth, she understood why he'd been wary of commitment. He'd been with Janine for four years, and it had all gone badly wrong—not through either of their fault. She could understand now why Lyle had said that Tyler's ex had broken his heart—but Janine's heart had been broken, too. The whole thing was so sad. "You're only human, Tyler. You need to forgive yourself."

"Maybe."

Even though she wasn't sure she wanted to hear the answer, she knew she had to ask the question. And she willed herself so hard not to stutter. She spoke very, very slowly. "Are you still in love with her?"

"I've had a year to get over her," he said.

Which wasn't quite answering her question. Saying you'd had time to get over someone wasn't the same as saying you weren't in love with them anymore. Did he still need more time? But she didn't feel she could push him any further. All she could do was reach over and squeeze his shoulder. "Are you still in t-touch with her?"

"No," he said. "She's moved on. And I need to do the same."

But there was a huge difference between knowing that you needed to move on, and actually doing it.

As if he'd guessed at her thoughts, he said, "I want to move on. With you."

For a second, she couldn't breathe.

He really wanted her?

"I know we haven't been together long and I'm probably rushing you." He dragged in a breath. "I'm sorry. I don't seem to be very good at relationships. I took it slowly with Janine and it went wrong. And now I'm rushing you and making a mess of things."

"It's fine," she said. "Thank you for sharing this with me. It won't go any further than me. And I don't know what to do or say to make you feel better, because anything I say could never be enough. But I'm sorry you both had to deal with something so tragic."

"Uh-huh." His voice was thick with emotion.

And all she could think of doing was to kiss him. To let him know she understood his emotions were all over the place.

And he kissed her back as if he were drowning and she was his lifeline.

"I don't want to mess things up between us," he said. "Bits of me want to carry you off to my bed, right now—but I don't want you thinking you're just a rebound fling and I'm using you for comfort because I told you about how bad things got with Janine. Because that's not how it is."

"Thank you." She stroked his face. "I'm not brilliant at relationships, either, So maybe we can learn together so... I don't know. So we trust ourselves to get it right, maybe."

"That sounds good to me."

She kissed him lightly.

"This isn't one of those 'it's not you, it's me' conversations," he said.

"I know." She'd had enough of those in the past to know the difference.

"Right now," he said, "all I want to do is hold you close."

"Me, too," she said, and wrapped her arms round him.

"We'll work this out," he said. "Together."

Chapter Ten

SATURDAY CAME ROUND all too soon. This time, the Bake-Off was taking place at the Main Street Diner. Beehive-haired Flo had agreed to let them use her ovens and was teasing all the bachelors about picking one of them as her next apprentice grill cook. Jodie Monroe was MCing the event again, and Jane McCullough had everyone organized.

The counter with its red leather-covered stools bolted to the floor in front of it was the setting for the Chinese auction lots; there were eight baskets representing each bachelor's favorite bits about Marietta. Tyler was truly grateful that Stacey had helped him put his basket together; thanks to her work with the cellophane and ribbons, it looked pretty.

One of the diner's waitresses was selling raffle tickets— the cloakroom type that had two strips of identical numbers per sheet. On the strip that stayed in the book, she was busy writing down names and telephone numbers on the back of each ticket, and gave the other strip to the person buying the tickets so they could place their tickets in the little plastic box in front of whichever baskets they wanted to win.

Everyone was filling up the tables, ready to watch the Bake-Off, and Tyler noticed that this time the elementary school's table seemed to have merged with the table containing staff and clients from Carter's Gym. Lyle Tate was there rather than at the fire crew's table—though that was probably because it meant he had more chance to chat with and charm half the women in the room. He caught Tyler's eye, winked, and made an L-shape on his forehead.

Tyler grinned and mimed aching muscles, earning him an answering grin and a thumbs-up from Lyle.

As before, the judges had their own little table; and for the duration of the Bake-Off the Diner was running a special menu of coffee, tea, sodas, and baked goods.

The eight bachelors assembled in front of their worktables, as directed by Jane, while Jodie Monroe introduced everyone and ran through what the bachelors would be baking and how the Chinese auction worked.

And then it was time to bake.

He glanced over at Stacey, who smiled at him, blew him a kiss, and mouthed "good luck—you've got this".

There were no eggs in the recipe, this time, so at least he wasn't going to drop any and have to borrow from his fellow bakers. But the memory of the over-sticky dough and the not-sticky-enough dough loomed large.

Please, this time, let him do Stacey's teaching justice.

He had to force himself to breathe properly as he measured out the ingredients for the dough, rubbed the butter into the flour, and added the water.

To his relief this time the dough worked out right and he managed to roll it without it sticking to the marble board or the wooden rolling pin. He sneaked a glance at the other bachelors to see how they were doing, and could see that Jake Price was struggling a bit. Jake looked up and exchanged a wry smile with him.

Funny, they were all so capable in their everyday jobs— but Tyler was aware that he wasn't the only one having trouble with this baking thing. He knew that it added to the fun for their audience and it meant that they were raising more money for Harry's House than if the bachelors had all been as accomplished at baking as Ryan Henderson or Rachel Vaughn. It was a good thing. But he for one was going to be glad when it was all over.

He carefully folded his pastry into quarters, the way Stacey had shown him. Then he placed the pastry into the pie dish. He held his breath in case the pastry split when he unfolded it, but it seemed to be going well. When he glanced up, Stacey caught his eye again and gave him an encouraging smile. Funny how she made him feel warm from the inside out.

He added the blueberry filling, then wetted the edge of the pastry on the pie dish as she'd shown him and put the lid on top. He looked round at his fellow bachelors and everyone seemed to be at a similar stage, which was reassuring. Maybe this was going to work out OK after all. He cut off the excess dough from the sides of the pie dish, crimped the edge, added steam holes on the top, said a silent prayer, and put his pie into the stove to cook.

While the pies were cooking, the final raffle tickets were sold for the Chinese auction baskets and the tickets were drawn to much whooping and catcalling.

And then it was time for the pies to come out.

To Tyler's horror, there was a crack across the top of the pie and the pastry had caught slightly at one edge. When something similar had happened at Stacey's, she'd simply smiled and told him to put ice cream on top, but he could hardly do that here.

He had to face it: he was going to come last. Again.

The judges came round to inspect the pies.

"I've got a ton more respect for what you do, now, Ry," Tyler said to Ryan Henderson. "Pastry's *hard*."

Ryan laughed. "I'm hoping that yours is buttery and crumbly, not hard."

Tyler smiled back. "Believe me, so am I—I just wish that edge hadn't caught."

"We're not going to taste that edge," Ryan said, "but you might want to prime someone to buy that slice for you at the auction afterward."

"Yeah."

"And it could've been worse," Ryan said. "We gave you a free choice of pie. We could've been really mean and made you make your own phyllo pastry."

"I don't think I want to know how you make phyllo pastry," Tyler said.

Ryan clapped him on the shoulder. "Come over to the shop someday, and I'll show you."

"If it means I get to eat it," Tyler said, "you're on."

The judges tasted each pie in turn and conferred with their score sheets. As before, Langdon Hale, the fire chief, stepped forward to announce the scores.

"Thanks to all our bachelors for again turning up and working so hard," he said. "And we're all agreed that the pies are delicious, so I hope everyone's going to bid generously for the slices when Jane auctions them off."

There was a general murmur of agreement from the audience.

"In eighth place, with brown sugar peach crumble, is Jake Price."

Tyler only then realized that he'd been holding his breath—and thank God this time he hadn't come last.

"In seventh place, with blueberry pie, is Tyler Carter."

The combined Marietta Elementary and Carter's Gym table erupted with wolf whistles and cheers.

Tyler could barely concentrate on the rest of the scores, though he noted that Zac Malone was the winner with blackberry and ginger pie.

Flo helped them all portion up the remainder of their pies and put them on paper plates covered with plastic wrap, and then Jane McCullough took over to auction off the pies.

Stacey and Kelly led the school and the gym to buy most of Tyler's pie, but when he spotted the piece with the burned crust he leapt in to bid for it. "Twenty dollars on top of whatever else is bid," he said.

And that piece was going straight in the bin.

"Seventh, this time. See? You're getting better," Stacey said when he went over to their table.

"Way to go, boss," Kelly said, and gave him a high five.

"And I'm assuming that my bet with your girl stands for this round, too," Lyle said. "So that's twenty dollars from me into the fund, and I have to sing something especially for you at my next FlintWorks gig, sugar—right?"

Stacey smiled. "Sounds good to me. I wish I'd said that you had to dress like Lady Gaga, too, as well as sing her song."

"I'd pay good money to see that," Tyler said.

"Me, too," Kelly added.

"And me," Tara said.

Lyle groaned. "Ladies—and Carter." He clutched both hands dramatically to his chest. "You wouldn't make me…"

They nodded in unison. "You bet we would."

Lyle looked at them. "If I do it—and I mean *if*—then it's going to cost you fifty dollars each," he said.

"For that much, you wear eyeliner and a dress," Kelly said.

"Just one tiny problem," Lyle said. "She wears a tuxedo in the video for that song."

"You don't wriggle out of it that easily. I'll get you a dress," Tara said.

"You could always borrow one from Carol Bingley," Kelly said with a grin. "Lyle, you're probably about the only person in town who could charm her into lending you a dress."

"This is getting out of hand," Lyle said. "So we'll compromise. I'll sing for lovely Stacey here, I'll wear eyeliner and a wig for Kelly, and I want a donation from you lot for Harry's House *and* a plate of buffalo wings and a beer after the gig."

"Deal," Kelly said, and shook his hand.

AFTERWARD, TYLER WAS smiling all the way back to their apartment block. "I can't wait for that FlintWorks gig. Kelly's going to enjoy finding him a wig. Something totally outrageous."

"And Lyle's a good sport. He'll wear it," Stacey said.

"Yeah. He's one of the good guys." Tyler hugged her. "I'm glad I didn't come last. I kind of feel I let you down, last week."

"No, you didn't. Baking's a new skill for you. You wouldn't expect me to be a first-class ice skater after that single lesson you gave me at the rink last week, would you?"

"Well, no," he admitted.

"Exactly—it's the same thing."

"Point conceded," he said. "So what do you want to do this evening? I would take you out to dinner, but as it's the nearest Saturday to Valentine's I think most places will already be fully booked."

"We don't need to go out. Could we do some more boxing?" she asked.

He was warmed all the way through that she actually liked what he'd been doing with her. Janine had never really been interested in his job. "Sure we can."

They stopped by her apartment so she could change into leggings, T-shirt, and sneakers, and then back at his apartment he pushed the furniture back to give them floor space and took her through the warm-up.

"One-two, punch from the shoulder, keep my arms up and my elbows down, and pivot for 'two'," she said, demonstrating the move. "Three-four is elbows up, and pivot."

"Great—let's do this."

"And we check my reach first," she said.

"Absolutely."

"And I punch *hard*."

"Yup."

She smiled when he started playing "Little Red Rooster". "Is this one of your chicken songs?"

"It's gone down very well in class," he said with a grin.

But he noticed that she was very focused and was frowning when she punched. He'd been there before on a one-to-one session, when his client had been seriously fed up about something and needed to blow off steam.

And he wondered…

Once he'd taken her through the cool down, he said, "Your punches were quite a bit harder today. Would I be right in guessing that you had someone in mind?"

She looked away. "Maybe."

"I can't imagine you wanting to punch anyone."

She wrinkled her nose. "Just sometimes."

He waited, and eventually she sighed. "OK. I had a text from my dad this morning, trying to guilt me into calling home."

"You don't call your parents?" He was surprised; he was close to his own family and spoke to them most days. The only reason his mom hadn't been the one to teach him to bake was because she and his dad were currently in New Zealand visiting her sister, and Lynnie lived an hour and a half's drive away in Billings and he'd persuaded her not to drive back to Marietta in the snow just to see him in the Bake-Off.

"I really d-don't enjoy using the phone," Stacey said. "I know my hearing aid is supposed to have a setting where I can hear the phone clearly, but it's never really worked for me and I end up having to use the loudspeaker to hear the other person talking. My father gets c-cross because he says there's too much interference and he can't hear me proper-ly." She shrugged. "So usually I text them, and it avoids the issue."

Tyler was seriously beginning to dislike Stacey's parents. If he'd been hearing-impaired, his parents would've made every effort to make life easier for him without making him feel like some special snowflake. They would've just worked round it and made sure he felt included. But Stacey's father seemed to be a bully who insisted on everything being done his way, and he didn't seem to be able to see what an amazing woman Stacey was.

"In your shoes," Tyler said, "I think I'd want to punch him, too."

"He's my dad," she said with a sigh, "and I'm s-supposed to love him and respect him. And I'm just as bad because I'm using my hearing impairment as an excuse not to call—the truth is, I just don't want to end up having another fight with him and disappointing him again."

How on earth could a woman like Stacey Allman possibly disappoint her parents? "He's your dad," Tyler said quietly, "and dads are meant to protect and support their daughters, not bully them. Plus respect has to be earned."

"I think he had a difficult childhood," Stacey said. "I don't really remember my grandparents, but my mom let a couple of things slip that made me think they gave him a hard time. And it's hard to be a parent when you don't have a good role model."

"You're a much nicer person than I am," Tyler said, "because my view is that if you don't know how to do something, you find someone who can teach you. You make the effort. Plus, if you've had a hard time as a kid, surely you want life to be better for your own kids and you treat them the way you wish you'd been treated?"

She looked awkward. "Ignore me. I shouldn't have said anything."

He held her close. "I'm sorry, too. It's not my place to criticize someone I've never even met. And it takes all sorts to make a world." He just wished that Stacey's father had been a bit kinder. She'd made the excuse for her father that he hadn't had a good role model; neither had Stacey, yet she still managed to be kind, sweet and caring and she stuck up for her students. Everything her father had failed to do for her.

"He's from a d-different generation," she said.

That still didn't excuse him, in Tyler's eyes. But he was glad that she'd at least had her aunt Joanie to bat her corner. "Maybe you could IM your parents instead of calling them—that way you don't have to struggle with hearing, and they still get the feel of a conversation," he suggested.

"I've tried that." She looked away. "They don't really like using a computer."

Give me strength, he thought. Could Stacey's parents not make one tiny bit of effort to help her? One little concession to make her life easier? "I have a couple of friends who are really good with technology," he said. "I could run the situation by them to see if they have any bright ideas?"

"Thanks, but I'll suck it up and call them. Like I said, I'm using my hearing impairment as an excuse. But maybe I'll wait until tomorrow to call them," Stacey said.

"OK." He kissed her lightly. "Come and have a shower with me—and then maybe we can order pizza and chill out with a movie."

"I'd like that," she said. "Can I grab some clothes from next door, first?"

"Sure you can." He paused. "And maybe you'd like to bring your pj's?"

Her eyes went wide. "Are you asking m-me to stay over?"

"Yes."

"OK."

She was gone a while, and Tyler was at the point of wondering if she'd changed her mind—but then she knocked on his door. When he answered, he could see that she'd brought her pajamas and toothbrush with her.

"Everything OK?" he asked.

"I, ah, had another message from my dad. So I returned the call."

He didn't push her to tell him everything. It was pretty obvious that it hadn't been a great conversation. Instead, he led her through his bathroom, gently removed all her clothes, and stepped with her into the shower. He lathered every inch of skin, cherishing her; but he could still feel the tension in her shoulders.

He dried her off just as tenderly and helped her into her

pajamas: a plain jersey camisole top with lacy edges, and trousers with little Scottie dogs on them. "Very cute," he said. "Like you."

She went slightly pink. "Sorry. I probably should've just stayed at my place and kept my grouchiness to myself."

"Absolutely not—let's order pizza and choose a movie."

They curled up on his sofa together under a fleecy blanket.

"Instead of a movie," he suggested, "we could watch a rerun of *Friends.*"

"Are you sure you wouldn't mind?" she asked.

"I'm sure," he said. "My sister always says that *Friends,* pizza, and hot chocolate makes even the roughest day feel OK again."

"She has a very good point."

To Tyler's relief, her smile reached her eyes. He grinned. "And I promise I won't make you eat the piece of pie I bid for."

"What's wrong with it?"

"Burned edges." He shook his head in puzzlement. "How can a pie just burn in *one* place?"

"It depends how you roll it, I guess," she said.

After they'd eaten pizza, he made her a mug of hot chocolate. Tucked up with him under the blanket on the sofa, with the hot chocolate and one of her all-time favorite episodes of *Friends* on his TV, Tyler thought that Stacey seemed way, way happier.

He made love to her very tenderly that night, and she fell asleep in his arms.

THE NEXT MORNING, Stacey woke in Tyler's bed, with her back to him; he was spooned round her body, holding her close. What now? Did she wait until he woke up, or did she wriggle out of bed? Should she go back to her own place while he was still asleep? She'd completely forgotten the etiquette about this kind of thing, and she felt slightly awkward until he kissed her bare shoulder. "Good morning."

He didn't sound in the slightest bit fazed, and that gave her confidence. She turned round to face him. "Good morning."

"I," he said, "am going to make you breakfast in bed. Stay put."

Given that he'd admitted to burning toast, she was pretty sure that breakfast wasn't going to involve anything actually cooked. But then he brought her a tray with a perfect mug of coffee—plus a glass of freshly squeezed orange juice, and a bowl of granola topped with Greek yoghurt and out-of-season strawberries.

"Wait—we need a finishing touch. I know it's not Valentine's until Tuesday, but…" He switched on his phone and held it out to her, and she could see a photograph of a single beautiful red rose.

She smiled at him. "That's so cute."

"I can hardly go and steal one from the communal garden—not in February," he said with a smile, "so this was the best option I could think of."

"It's lovely—thank you. I feel really spoiled."

STACEY CLEARLY WASN'T used to the men she dated treating her like this, Tyler thought, whereas Janine had pretty much taken for granted that he'd always bring her breakfast in bed on a Sunday morning if he wasn't working. He'd thought that Janine was the love of his life, but now he was beginning to think he'd been wrong; every day he was falling a little bit more in love with Stacey, with her sweetness and kindness.

After breakfast, she helped him wash up. "So are you working the late shift today?" she asked.

"Yes."

"Are you up for a baking lesson this morning? The last Bake-Off involves cake, right?"

"Right—and yes, I'd love a lesson, as long as it's not layer cake." Though the one good thing about that mess of an afternoon was that he'd met Stacey properly.

She laughed. "No, I think we decided on a glazed cake, didn't we? The one I normally bake is lemon, but we can make it an orange one so it's that little bit different."

"Let's do it."

He liked the calm, quiet way she went about her kitchen, finding the equipment and getting all the ingredients out.

"Do we have to preheat the stove?" he asked.

"We do indeed," she said, "to 350 degrees. I haven't had time to get the butter to room temperature, so just ignore what I'm about to do," she added, "because this bit's very easy to get wrong—and this won't happen at the Bake-Off anyway, because they'll make sure your ingredients are at room temperature rather than straight from the fridge."

She put a stick of butter in the mixing bowl, popped it in the microwave for a few seconds, then tested the butter with a knife.

"You cooked the butter?" he asked.

"I've just softened it for you," she said, "but it's easy to go too far, and once it's melted you're going to find it hard to cream the butter with the sugar."

"Got you—and creaming the butter and sugar's the same as we did for the cookies, right?"

"Nope," she said, "because this time you'll use my hand mixer. The idea is to get as much air as possible into the mixture, so you keep beating it until it's pale and fluffy."

On her instructions, he added three quarters of a cup of powdered sugar plus a teaspoon to the bowl.

She clicked the beaters into place and handed him the cordless hand mixer. "Keep it on a low setting, at first," she said.

He really meant to put the mixer on the first setting, but

somehow he accidentally made it to third and the sugar shot out of the bowl and went all over her worktop.

He looked at her, horrified—but she was laughing.

"That was a learning opportunity," she said. "Now you know why I said to keep it on low."

"I can't believe I've messed it up already," he said ruefully.

"Don't worry about it. I'll rescue this and make it into something later. Let's try again." She kissed him, then took out another glass mixing bowl and softened the butter for him.

He added the sugar to the bowl and this time kept the mixer on low; once the butter and sugar were amalgamated, on her instructions he increased the setting and kept beating the mixture until it was pale and fluffy.

"Now you add some orange rind," she said, and handed him an orange and a box grater. "Keep it light, because you just want the rind and the oils, not the pith. You'll squeeze the rest of the orange to make the glaze."

He grated rind into the bowl, then beat the batter again quickly.

"Now beat two eggs in a bowl and add them," she said.

He took his time cracking the eggs into a small bowl, and managed to do it without getting bits of shell among the eggs, then added the eggs to the cake batter.

"Fold in one and a half cups of flour and three teaspoons of baking powder—you do it with a metal spoon," she said, "so you don't take the air out that you've just spent ages putting in."

"Fold?" he asked.

"Like this," she said, and showed him. "Round and down."

Once he'd stirred in the flour, she said, "Now you can add the milk, a tablespoon at a time. You want what my aunt Joanie calls a dropping consistency—all that means is the batter will drop off the spoon when you shake it gently."

"And if I add too much milk?" he asked, remembering the mess he'd made by adding too much liquid to the pastry.

"That's why you do it one at a time and test it after each one," she said with a smile.

It took four tablespoons to get the right consistency.

"Now you pour the batter into a loaf tin—and this is where I cheat because I use a ready-made liner instead of cutting baking parchment."

"Will I be allowed to do that at the Bake-Off?"

"I don't see why not. And once the batter's spread out evenly, you bake it for forty to fifty minutes," she said.

Five minutes before the cake was due to come out of the stove, she helped him juice the orange and added two tablespoons of granulated sugar to the bowl. "Stick it in the microwave for about thirty seconds," she said, "so the sugar dissolves in the juice."

Then she showed him how to test the cake with a skewer so it came out clean with no cake batter sticking to it.

"This is the glaze part. You stick the skewer very gently into the top of the cake, so the glaze sinks in more easily, then spoon the orange syrup over the top and let the cake cool in the tin."

He did what she suggested, then stared at the finished result. It actually *looked* like a cake. "You're awesome," he said.

When she brushed his praise aside, he said, "No, really— I mean it, Stacey. You're amazing. You're kind and you're bright and I can't believe how much difference you've made to my world in the last couple of weeks. Without you, I'd be really dreading this Bake-Off thing, but you've made it fun. And I feel as if I could tackle something in the kitchen now, instead of backing away because I've been so hopeless in the past."

"You," she said, "are very far from hopeless. Look at the way you skate."

"You know what I mean. And you've inspired me on the kids' class project. I never would have thought about it without you—that I can help make life a little bit less of a struggle for vulnerable kids. We're a good team." He kissed her. "You're amazing, Stacey. Never let anyone make you feel otherwise." Especially, he thought, your father. Because he clearly doesn't have a clue.

He took the cake to work.

"Marry her *now*," Kelly demanded after the first taste. Tyler laughed it off, but the words stuck in his head all afternoon. Except it was nothing to do with the way Stacey baked, and everything to do with the way she made him feel.

STACEY THOUGHT ABOUT what Tyler had said during the afternoon. She wouldn't describe herself as amazing; but she also wasn't the dumb, useless person her father always made her feel that she was.

And maybe it was finally time to do something about that.

She picked up the phone and called him.

"Why are you calling?" he asked. "We spoke yesterday."

"I know. That's why I'm c-calling, Dad." She took a deep breath. Now wasn't the time to stutter. She wanted him to hear her words, not nitpick about her delivery. "I love you, but I don't like the way you treat me, so I'm not coming to Missoula the weekend after next. I don't see the point of driving for nearly four hours to visit you, only for you to make me feel bad, the second I walk in the door."

"That's ridiculous. Stacey, you're so d—"

"Stop, Dad," she cut in. "If you were going to say 'dumb', you know it's not true. I graduated top of my class. I'm hearing-impaired and I have a stutter, yes, but I'm not stupid."

"You're wasting your degree, working in a backwater school in a little hick town," he snarled.

"Marietta isn't a hick town," she said. "It's beautiful out here. Which you'd know if you and Mom had ever bothered to come and see me or Aunt Joanie."

He snorted. "Joanie's a bad influence on you."

"You mean, she stands up to you."

"I don't know what's got into you, Stacey Allman."

"I've finally grown a backbone," she said. "And I'm not prepared to listen to you putting me down all the time. Why do you need to do it, Dad? Why do you always tell me I'm useless and stupid?"

"So you'll fight back and prove me wrong."

It was the last thing she'd been expecting. And she wasn't sure if it made her feel more hurt or angry. Did he really think she was that easy to manipulate? "As a schoolteacher, I can tell you that's not the most helpful psychology," she said. "And, on a personal note, before I do anything new, I hear your voice telling me that I'm going to fail. And I have to get past that every single time before I can move on."

"Are you blaming m—?" he began.

"No, Dad, I'm explaining how what you say actually affects me—you might not mean it, but it's how it is," she cut in. "I want things to be different in the future. I want to be able to enjoy a visit with my parents, like normal people do, instead of dreading it because I know that I'm a constant disappointment to you and you're going to make sure I know it." She took a deep breath. "Maybe I wasn't planned, but if you and Mom really hadn't wanted me disrupting your life, then maybe you should've given me up for adoption to someone who *did* actually want me."

For the first time she could ever remember, her father was silent.

"And that," she said, "is why I'm not coming to Missoula, the weekend after next. If you really want to see me and have a proper relationship with me, you know where I am."

And then, very gently, she cut the connection.

Her hands were shaking, but she felt better than she had in a long, long time. She'd finally stood up to her father and told him what she wanted to change in her relationship with her parents. And she knew exactly why she'd finally had the confidence to do it: Tyler. He'd taught her that she *could* do things, that she wasn't automatically going to fail. Boxing, ice-skating, standing up to her parents... She could do it. Do it all.

Chapter Eleven

O<small>N MONDAY, STACEY</small> called in to see her aunt Joanie on the way home from school.

"I hear you spoke to your father yesterday," Joanie said.

Stacey winced. "Ah. Mom called you?"

"Yes." Joanie gave her a hug. "Well done. It's about time you stood up to Charles."

"I feel guilty," Stacey admitted. "It isn't like me to be mean to people."

"You weren't mean, honey, you just told him the truth—and don't back down," Joanie said. "You stand your ground. You're in the right."

Stacey grimaced. "Dad might never speak to me again."

"Which will be his loss, not yours. He'll think about it," Joanie said, "and he might huff and puff a bit and he definitely won't tell you that he's sorry, but he'll realize you just spoke the truth." She paused. "I hear you're seeing Tyler Carter."

"It's early days," Stacey hedged.

"He's a good man, from what I hear." Joanie patted

Stacey's shoulder. "It's good to see you looking happy."

And yes, she was happy. She loved her job, she loved Marietta, and she was definitely falling in love with the man next door.

THAT EVENING, STACEY knocked on Tyler's door. "Are you too busy, or can I take you out for a drink at FlintWorks?"

"For you, I'm never too busy," he said, and smiled. "Any special reason?"

"I owe you, because you've helped give me a backbone." She explained what had happened with her father.

"The backbone is all you," Tyler said, "and good for you. Even if he's mad about it right now, give him time to think about what you said and he'll come round."

"I'm not so sure. He's pretty stubborn," Stacey said.

"I'm guessing he just needed a wake-up call, and now he's got it. Let me grab my jacket and my car keys."

"No need. I'm driving *you*," she said. "So you can have a beer without worrying about being over the limit."

"I'd like that. A beer with my girl. Thank you." He stole a kiss. "Tomorrow's Valentine's. I feel bad that I'm not going to be able to take you out, because I'm on late shift at the gym."

"It's fine," she said. "I have book group tomorrow, anyway. And we're discussing a romantic comedy."

He still felt guilty, though. Maybe he could arrange some surprises for her.

But in the end Tuesday turned out to be manic at work, and he didn't have time to think about something nice to do for Stacey before all the stores were closed.

And when Tyler opened his front door after work, he stopped dead as he saw Janine sitting on the couch.

He opened his mouth to ask what she was doing there, but no words came out.

"I still had my key," she said. "I hope you don't mind—I didn't know where else to go."

He closed the door behind him, frowning. "I thought you were living in Billings?"

"I was."

Then he saw the traces of tears on her face. Clearly something was very wrong. But why had she come here? Why hadn't she gone to her mom's in Bozeman?

He raked a hand through his hair. "I'll make us some coffee."

"Just a glass of water for me, please."

Something was definitely wrong—in the years they'd lived together, he'd always joked that Janine had pure caffeine instead of blood in her veins. Grimly, he made himself an espresso and poured her a glass of water.

"So what's happened?" he asked.

And that was when she started crying.

What else could he do but go over to her and put his

arms around her? They'd been together for nearly five years. OK, so their breakup had fractured his heart, and they weren't together anymore—but he couldn't just stand there and watch her cry her heart out.

There was a huge wet patch on his shoulder by the time she'd stopped shuddering, but he could live with that.

"What's happened?" he asked again.

"I got that job in Billings," she said.

"Managing a large hotel." He remembered. She'd seen it as a step toward managing a chain.

"And the guy who owned the hotel chain… He dropped in a lot, to see how I was settling in." She dragged in a breath. "One thing led to another, and we started seeing each other."

Tyler was pretty sure this story wasn't going to have a happy ending.

"I thought he was separated," Janine continued.

Yup. Definitely not a happy ending.

"And then…" She dragged in a breath. "I went off coffee."

He went cold. He remembered the one time when that had happened before. "You're pregnant?"

She nodded.

He tried to keep his voice as measured as possible, because the memories coming back to him felt as if someone had slugged him hard in the gut. "How pregnant are you?"

"Thirteen weeks."

Past the date when everything had gone so badly wrong for them. Which was a good thing—for her sake, he hoped that history wouldn't repeat itself.

But the fact that she was thirteen weeks pregnant, in tears, and had used her old key to their apartment... It all added up to things not going so well when she'd told her lover that she was expecting their baby. The fact that she hadn't turned to her mom told him pretty much the rest of the story.

"I take it he's not standing by you and the baby?"

She shook her head and looked away. "He told me he was separated. But when I told him about the baby, he said he was getting back together with his wife." She took a deep breath. "Then he said he wanted me to get rid of it."

Tyler blew out a breath. "That's..." He didn't have the words to express how he felt. No matter what your views on termination, surely you wouldn't expect that from someone who'd been through the harrowing misery of a miscarriage?

"So I left," she said.

Tyler had a feeling that there was more to it than that. "He sacked you, or you quit?"

"I couldn't work there anymore. Not knowing that he'd lied to me and wanted me to...to..." She shuddered. "So I left. This morning."

"OK." He paused. "What about your mom?"

"I took the train back to Bozeman—my car belonged to the hotel so I lost that along with my job. I took a taxi from the train station in Bozeman back to Mom's. But when I told her everything…" Janine swallowed hard. "I suppose it brought back memories of all the time my dad cheated on her. And she said there was no way I could stay with her, not when I was pregnant by a married man."

Tyler winced inwardly. There was always more than one side to a story, and surely you always put your kids first? Or maybe he and Lynnie had been super-lucky with the best parents ever.

"So that's why I took a taxi back to Marietta. Can I stay here?" she asked.

Pregnant and alone, with nowhere else to go. Of course he wasn't going to be cruel and turn her away tonight—he wouldn't turn anyone away who needed help like this. Obviously staying here wasn't going to be a permanent thing; tomorrow he would take some time off work and help her to find somewhere to live and maybe a job, either here or in Bozeman. And, although he didn't have the greatest relationship with Janine's mom, he might call her and try to broker peace between them.

"Of course you can stay," he said. His sense of decency made him add, "And you can have my bed. I'll sleep on the sofa."

"I kind of left Mom's without taking much with me," she admitted. "Could I borrow a shirt to sleep in?"

"Sure."

Tyler knew he needed to tell Stacey about this—and he

probably ought to tell Janine that he was involved with someone else. But diplomatically. And right now he thought she might be too upset to take it in.

"I'll just go and change the sheets," he said, and headed off to his bedroom to sort out the bed linen.

Stacey was at book club tonight, he was pretty sure, but he texted her swiftly. *Need to talk to you—Janine just arrived at my apartment. She needs my help. I can't just turn her away. Can we talk tomorrow?* He pressed "send", then concentrated on changing the bed linen before going back to Janine.

"Have you had anything to eat?" he asked.

She shook her head. "I felt too upset and too sick."

"OK—but you do need to eat." For her own sake as well as the baby's. "What can you eat that doesn't make you feel bad?"

"Something plain, like pasta." She looked at him. "I'm guessing you still don't cook?"

"No. But I can order plain pasta from Rocco's," he said. "Anything else?"

"Maybe some chicken? But no sauce, please, and definitely nothing with garlic." She shuddered.

"OK. Go and make yourself comfortable," he said. "I've left you some clean towels on the bed. Feel free to use whatever you need in the bathroom."

"Thank you, Tyler." She took a deep breath. "This is way more than I deserve, after the way I treated you."

"It takes two to break a relationship," he said, remembering what Stacey had said to him. "We were both at fault for what happened."

"Even so. I'm sorry I dumped myself on you tonight, but I didn't know where else to go and you were the only person I could think of who might help me."

"Don't worry. We can sort something out." He'd have a think about where she could stay—if need be, he'd pay for her to stay at the Bramble House B&B—and another think about where she might be able to get a job.

When he ordered plain pasta and chicken from Rocco's, he thought back to the last takeout he'd ordered from there with Stacey, sharing dough balls and laughing. But, given that Janine's relationship had ended so badly, he wasn't going to rub her nose in it by telling her how much happiness he'd found with Stacey. He made another call to Sam, arranging to swap shifts so he could go in early and finish at lunchtime, giving him the afternoon to help Janine find somewhere to live. And he spent the evening chatting to her, trying to be as kind as he could.

But all the time he was waiting for his phone to buzz with a text from Stacey. He knew she had a good heart and she'd understand that he really had to help Janine, but it bothered him a bit that she didn't reply. Or maybe the book club was particularly noisy tonight and she hadn't heard her phone beep to signal a message?

She still hadn't replied by the late evening. Maybe she'd gone out for a drink with the book club group after they'd discussed whatever they were reading, he thought, or maybe she felt it was a bit too late to text him back.

Once he was sure Janine was settled, he made himself a bed on his sofa—but it was a long while before he could get to sleep.

Seeing Janine again had stirred up all the memories of how badly he'd got his last relationship wrong. Had he learned enough for things to go right with Stacey? Or would he end up repeating his mistakes with her?

IT WAS A bit strange that Tyler hadn't texted her, Stacey thought. Even though she'd been at the book group last night, she'd half expected him to check his shifts and suggest times for baking practice during the week. Or, if he'd been planning to try making a cake on his own, as he had with the cookies and the pie, surely he would've asked her when she was free to be his taste tester? Plus he'd had that ridiculous bee in his bonnet over yesterday being Valentine's. She hadn't expected him to send her flowers or a card, but she had kind of expected a text.

So was something wrong?

She was pretty sure that he was on a late shift, that day, so she knocked on his door just before she left for school.

To her surprise, a woman answered the door, wearing nothing but a man's flannel shirt—a shirt that Stacey recognized as belonging to Tyler.

The woman was tall and voluptuous, with perfectly straight dark hair and huge brown eyes. She didn't look anything like Tyler, so Stacey was pretty sure this wasn't his sister Lynnie. So who was the mystery woman?

"Uh, um…" To her horror, she couldn't even get a word out.

"Yes?" the other woman asked.

Stacey took a deep breath and willed herself to stay calm. She was absolutely sure that Tyler wasn't a louse and he would have a very good reason for a gorgeous woman being in his apartment, almost naked except for an item of his clothing. "I'm S-Stacey from next door."

"Good to meet you. I'm Janine," the other woman said with a smile.

Janine? As in his ex?

Though it figured. Hadn't Lyle Tate said that Tyler's ex was stunning? The woman standing in the doorway was utterly gorgeous, tall and slender yet curvy at the same time. Even wearing nothing but a man's shirt, she managed to look stylish.

But Janine didn't seem to notice that Stacey hadn't said a word.

"I don't think you were here when I lived here before," Janine said.

"No. I m-moved here over the summer," Stacey explained.

"Well, I'm sure we'll get to know each other now I'm back," Janine said with a smile. "Sorry, I would invite you in for coffee, but…" She gestured to the way she was dressed.

The implication was very, very clear.

Tyler's ex was back. Wearing Tyler's shirt. Which meant there was a very strong likelihood that Tyler was in his bedroom, wearing even less.

How could she have been so stupid? "It's fine." Right now Stacey didn't want to go into Tyler's apartment for coffee—or for anything else.

"Did you want me to give Ty a message for you?"

"I… N-no. It's fine. It was nothing important." And it was pretty obvious that she was surplus to requirements for the Bake-Off, now.

"Oh. Well, I'll tell him you called round."

"Th-thanks."

Stacey headed out to her car, feeling dazed. Yesterday, she'd been dating Tyler. Today, his ex was back in town and had clearly stayed at his apartment last night—how ironic, on Valentine's Day—and she was wearing Tyler's shirt, so it looked as if they were back together. Tyler obviously hadn't told Janine that he'd been seeing Stacey. With an aching heart, Stacey wondered just when Tyler had intended to tell her that it was over between them because Janine was back.

Stacey, you're so dumb. The words echoed through her head—and to think at the weekend she'd told her father that wasn't true. It looked as if her dad was absolutely right, after all. How stupid she'd been to think things would work out between her and someone as gorgeous as Tyler Carter. Of course he'd rather be with someone like Janine—a woman who was tall and beautiful and voluptuous, instead of short and mousy and ordinary.

And it wasn't as if he'd declared himself in love with Stacey. When he'd told her about Janine, she'd asked him straight out if he was still in love with his ex, and he hadn't denied it. He'd simply said that he'd had a year to get over her: which wasn't the same thing at all as saying that he was actually over her.

Still brooding, Stacey drove to school. Though she wished she hadn't turned on the radio when she heard Dolly Parton plaintively begging Jolene not to take her man.

Even the names sounded similar: Jolene and Janine.

Except, strictly speaking, Tyler was Janine's man. Had been for years. She was the love of his life.

Which left Stacey precisely one option: to back off gracefully. And, even though she loved her apartment, she'd maybe start looking round for somewhere else to live that wasn't right next to Tyler and the love of his life.

She parked at school, took a deep breath, and reminded herself to leave her personal life outside the elementary school buildings. And then she walked into her classroom, ready to teach her kindergarten children.

TYLER CHECKED HIS phone for the tenth time that morning. There was still no reply from Stacey.

OK, so she'd be in lessons right now, or maybe in a meeting, depending on whether it was a teaching day or a coordination day.

But he really needed to talk to her and tell her about Janine turning up unexpectedly last night, and explain the situation, before someone like Carol Bingley found out that Janine was back, got the wrong idea, and spread all kinds of rumors over town. Stacey was the walking definition of kindness, so she might even have some good ideas about who might have a place for Janine to stay or where there might be a job going—not that he thought Janine would stay here too long anyway, because she never really had settled in Marietta.

In the end he asked Kelly to cover his class for him and headed over to the elementary school, hoping to catch Stacey before she went to lunch.

He charmed the school secretary into letting him in. "I know I'm asking a lot because I don't have all the clearances and what have you to be in a school, but I really need a quick and fairly urgent word with Miss Allman."

"About the Bake-Off? In that case, I think I can turn a blind eye," the secretary said with a smile.

Not correcting her was equivalent to lying, and Tyler felt guilty. But he was running short on options and he really needed to see Stacey. Besides, maybe they could talk about the Bake-Off for all of two seconds.

"What you're all doing in Harry Monroe's name is wonderful," the secretary said, and gave him directions to Stacey's classroom.

As Tyler walked through the corridors, he could see through each classroom door that the children had already gone to the main hall for their lunch. So there was a fair chance that Stacey would be free, even if it was only for a couple of minutes.

He paused outside Stacey's classroom and knocked on the open door.

She looked up and her beautiful blue-grey eyes went wide as she saw him.

What he wanted to do right then, more than anything else, was to run over to her, pick her, up, whirl her round, and kiss her until they were both senseless. But he knew that was way, way too inappropriate for an elementary school. Instead, he said, "Hey, Stacey."

"T-tyler." She took a deep breath. "I wasn't expecting t-to see you."

He frowned. "But I texted you last night."

She frowned back. "I didn't get any text from you."

Oh, great. The one time he really needed his cell phone company to deliver the message, the system had let him down. "I'm sorry. I know it's your lunchtime, and you really need a break, but I think we need to talk."

"There's no n-need," she said brightly. "I already saw Janine this morning."

"So you know—"

"I know," she cut in. "If you'll excuse me, I'm about t-to go into a meeting."

A nasty thought struck him. Had she actually talked to Janine and found out why his ex had returned to Marietta? Or had she made an assumption that Janine hadn't corrected?

He knew her confidence in herself was rock bottom, thanks to her dad. But surely she knew him well enough to realize that he would never, ever just dump her for his ex? Surely she had an idea how he felt about her?

But he could see her backing away.

Fast.

And he knew she wasn't going to listen to anything he said. It'd be filtered through her lack of confidence and what she'd hear would be nothing like what he meant. And of course she'd want to protect herself. She'd push him away and build a massive brick wall round herself.

He had a nasty feeling that the only way he could fix this was to get Janine to come with him and explain. Properly. Plus she'd said she was about to go into a meeting. He wasn't entirely sure whether it was an excuse or she really did have a meeting, but now wasn't the place to press the point. He'd regroup and try and talk to her again later. "OK," he said. "I'll catch you later."

She gave him the brittlest, brittlest smile that didn't even begin to reach her eyes. "Sure."

He made a point of thanking school secretary for her help on his way out, and called Warren Hunt at the Graff on his way back to the apartment block.

"Good to hear from you, Carter. Is this about the Bake-Off on Saturday?" Warren asked.

"No, it's more of a personal thing," Tyler said. "I'm trying to help a friend. I just wondered if you knew of any hotel that's hiring staff at management level right now?"

"Not here in Marietta," Warren said. "What kind of distance would your friend be willing to travel? I could have a word with some contacts in Livingston or Bozeman, if you like."

"That," Tyler said gratefully, "would be wonderful. Thank you."

"No problem."

"I would offer you a free month's membership at my place to say thanks properly," Tyler said, "except I know you go to Lane Scott's gym and I'm not in the poaching business."

Warren laughed. "I know, and it's fine. I'll call you later."

Back at his apartment, Janine was dressed in the clothes she'd worn the previous day, except they'd clearly been washed and ironed.

"I did the laundry," she said cheerfully. "And the ironing."

"You really didn't need to do that," he said.

"It's the least I can do, since you're letting me stay. I hope you don't mind, but I'm going to pop out and get some new clothes. I'll cook dinner tonight."

Tyler knew that she hated cooking as much as he did. They'd always eaten out or bought takeout. All this domesticity and the fact she hadn't mentioned how long she wanted to stay… It sounded to him as if Janine wanted to stay at his apartment for the foreseeable future.

And then a really nasty thought struck him. She'd said she'd turned to him because she had nowhere else to go. She didn't think they were going to start up again where they'd left off, did she?

He needed to put her straight about Stacey. Fast.

"Janine, we need to talk," he said. "And I swapped my duty over so I could have the afternoon off to help you find somewhere to live and maybe a job."

"I can't go looking for a job without new clothes," she said. "Catch you later." And she scooted out of the front door before he could say anything else.

Oh, hell. She'd picked up on what he'd said about the job but not about finding her a place to live. Clearly she thought he was single and she could stay here indefinitely.

What was he going to do?

He felt sorry for Janine, and of course he'd help her out of trouble. But he wasn't in love with her anymore; and he had no chance of making Stacey see how he felt about her if Janine was still living with him.

And he knew Janine wouldn't be happy here in Marietta. Not for long. She was a city girl through and through.

Which left him little choice.

The last time he'd spoken to Janine's mother, it had been unpleasant in the extreme. He'd just have to deal with it. He wished he had Lyle Tate's easy charm, but in the end all he could do was be himself. Be honest. And hope that would be enough.

He called Marie's cell phone.

She answered, sounding suspicious and clearly not recognizing the number. "Who is this?"

Here came Armageddon. "It's Tyler Carter."

"What the hell do you want?" she asked.

"To talk to you."

"Well, I don't want to talk to—"

"—about Janine," he cut in.

"She's with you?"

"No. She's currently in town, buying new clothes, as she didn't have anything with her when she arrived last night."

"You know what she's done?"

He sighed. "Yes. She told me."

"And you're still letting her stay with you?"

"She's pregnant, alone, and in a mess. What would any decent human being do, Marie? We were together for nearly five years. I know it was bad at the end, but it takes two to break a relationship. And I'm not going to turn my back on someone I once loved."

"Oh." She sounded faintly guilty, which gave Tyler hope.

"You and I both know she won't settle in Marietta. Janine hates small towns. She might stick it out for a few weeks, a few months, or maybe even until the baby arrives. But then she's going to feel trapped," Tyler said, "and what she really needs is her family. Her mother. Someone who's been there, who's had to struggle with all the difficulties a single mom faces. Someone who's done it successfully."

"Are you flattering me?" Marie demanded.

"No. I'm telling it like it is. Putting aside whatever disagreements you and I had in the past, I always admired your guts in bringing Janine up on your own. The way you didn't take any nonsense from anyone."

"The father of her baby is married to someone else. She knew he was married when she started seeing him." Tyler could hear the anger in Marie's tone. "I can't condone that."

"I'm not asking you to condone it. But I'm pretty sure the guy lied to her and told her he was separated. Janine's got your moral backbone, Marie. She would have turned him down if she'd thought he was still with his wife—even if it meant losing her job under some stupid pretext he thought up." He paused. "Which is pretty much what's happened to her."

"I guess."

"She needs you, Marie. Much more than she thinks she needs me. And I'm not trying to dump my responsibilities on you," Tyler said. "I'm seeing someone else. Someone I think I have a real future with. I can't give Janine what she thinks she wants, because we're not in love with each other and it'd be a huge mistake to get back together."

"That's true."

"I've got friends talking to their contacts to see if I can help find her a job. Hopefully there will be something in Bozeman."

"And you want her to come back and live with me?"

"I think," he said, "you're exactly what she needs. Her mom. The woman who's been in her shoes and can reassure her that there's light at the end of the tunnel."

Marie sighed. "You're right, dammit. As you say, you and I haven't always seen eye to eye. But I think you've got my girl's best interests at heart."

"Yours, too," he said. "Of course you're angry with her. She's in a situation that's brought back bad memories for you, and that's hard for you. But if you let that anger come between you, if you let it push her away, then sooner or later you're going to wake up and regret it. You'll hate yourself. And," he added, "you'll miss out on those first few precious days of a baby. Your grandchild."

"You should've been a diplomat," she said.

He laughed. "That's pretty much what any personal trainer has to be."

"All right. So you want me to come and pick her up?"

"No, it's OK. I'll bring her home to you," he said.

"Tomorrow," she said. "I'll be home all day."

"I'll text you when we leave," he said. "And thank you, Marie."

"It's what a mom's for," she said. "And it took you to remind me of that. So I probably owe you thanks."

"Let's call it quits," he said. "See you tomorrow."

Just after he'd disconnected the call, Warren rang with details of a contact in Bozeman who might be able to offer Janine a job.

So he'd found her a place to live and hopefully somewhere to make a living.

Now all he had to do was tell her.

Chapter Twelve

"I'M NOT GOING back to Mom's," Janine said. "Absolutely not."

"I talked to her. She understands better now."

"You had no right." She stared at him. "Who asked you to interfere?"

He narrowed his eyes at her. "You came here asking for my help. Which is what you've got."

"I just wanted a place to stay."

"You've got one. With your mom," he pointed out.

She shook her head. "I'm not going back to my mom's. But I'm clearly not welcome here, so—"

He took her hand. "Janine, you've had a rough week. A really, really rough week. You expected your mom to be there for you, and she wasn't. But she is now. And it'll all be OK."

Janine looked anguished. "I can't stay with her. She hates me."

"She hates what she thought you did," he corrected. "She loves you. She's going to love your baby."

"Is she?"

"When you lost our baby, we weren't the only ones who grieved," he reminded her. "Your mom wants you. Really, she does. And you'd be much happier in Bozeman than you would be here," he added gently. "You hated it here before. Marietta hasn't changed."

"Maybe I've changed."

He looked at the power suit she was wearing—something totally unsuitable for a small town in a Montana winter. She was a city girl through and through. "Really?"

She shrugged, realizing what he was getting at. "So I like nice clothes."

"It's not just about the clothes. It's about the difference between a small town and a city. It's about the people."

"You don't want me here." She started to cry.

The woman he'd fallen in love with had been tough, and she definitely hadn't been manipulative. Either Janine really had changed in the last year, or this was hormones taking over and making her act out of character. He had to force himself to be patient. "My life's different now." He paused. "I believe you met my neighbor this morning."

"Oh, the mousy little thing with a stutter. Yes. I don't know why she came round. She didn't leave a message."

Mousy little thing with a stutter? That so wasn't who Stacey was. And that one catty comment tried his patience to breaking point. He dropped Janine's hand as if it had burned him. "Stacey's a good friend."

"What?" Janine stared at him, and her eyes went wide as she saw the expression on his face and clearly jumped to the right conclusion. "You're kidding. You and *her?* She's not your type."

Oh, but she was. "I think," he said, "this conversation had better stop right now, for both our sakes. And I'm driving you to Bozeman tomorrow." And he'd change the locks on his apartment. He wasn't risking a situation like this happening ever, ever again.

THE NEXT MORNING, Stacey was about to drive off to school when she saw Tyler walk out of their apartment block, with Janine next to him.

Except neither of them looked very happy.

They weren't holding hands, and they didn't look as if they were walking right next to the love of their life.

Forget it and move on, she told herself sharply. This is none of your business, Stacey Allman.

Except she could see Tyler's mouth moving—and she could lip-read everything he was saying.

This was bad. It was the equivalent of eavesdropping. Nothing good would come of it, she knew.

But she couldn't stop herself doing it.

"We can't go back," he was saying. "I'm sorry. It was over between us more than a year ago. You made that very clear."

Stacey glanced at Janine.

"I made a mistake. I was wrong. Let me come back. I'll change."

"You weren't happy when you were with me before," Tyler said.

"Because we lost the baby," Janine protested. "This time, I'll make more of an effort."

"That's the whole point." He raked his hand through his hair. "If you really wanted to be with me, you wouldn't *need* to make an effort."

Stacey stared at them. So Janine wanted him back, but Tyler didn't want her back?

And then they both turned the corner and Stacey couldn't lip-read anymore.

She stayed where she was for a moment, her mind whirling. So had she got it all wrong? Was Janine not actually the love of Tyler's life? But, in that case, why was Janine staying with Tyler in Marietta?

Then again, Tyler had come to the school to talk to her, but she hadn't heard him out; thinking that he wanted Janine, she'd pushed him away. He'd said that he'd texted her—and, although she'd never actually received a text, it didn't mean that he hadn't sent it in the first place.

So maybe the conclusion she'd jumped to—that he'd dumped her, the second his ex came back, but hadn't bothered telling her—was completely wrong.

And in that case she owed him an apology.

If it wasn't too late.

TYLER'S CAR WASN'T in the parking lot that evening.

Or on Friday morning.

Maybe Tyler and Janine had had a heart-to-heart in the car, wherever they'd been traveling, and had made it up.

Stacey went to school as usual, and kept a smile on her face all day; and even though she ended up in a meeting with a seriously difficult parent, she kept her cool and fought in her student's corner.

That evening, there was a knock at her door. She answered it to discover Tyler standing on her doorstep, looking bone-deep weary, and her heart went out to him. Even though he'd hurt her, he was clearly upset about something and it just wasn't in her to shove him away. "Are you OK?" she asked.

"Thank you for asking. Probably not," he said.

"I take it Janine's not with you?" she asked carefully.

"She's in Bozeman, with her mom. And these are for you." He took his hands from behind his back and handed her the most gorgeous bouquet of deep red roses.

"But…"

"It's to say sorry," he said. "I did try to talk to you, but not hard enough."

"I need to say sorry, too—because I didn't let you talk to me. Come in," she said. "I don't have any beer, but I can pour you a glass of wine."

"Thanks. I could really do with it," he said.

She poured them both a glass of wine, then put the flowers in water. "Have you eaten?" she asked.

He shook his head.

"Neither have I. Go sit down. Dinner will be ten minutes." Thankfully she had a bag of stir-fry veg in the fridge, along with a pack of chicken tenders, and she always kept a packet of noodles, and a jar of stir-fry sauce in her cupboard.

Ten minutes later, she served them both a plate of stir-fry. "Sorry, I don't have any fortune cookies."

"I think mine would say 'you need to try harder'," Tyler said apologetically. "When you didn't reply to my original text, I should've realized that something was wrong and followed it up with a second text, or just called you."

"And I think mine would say 'don't jump to conclusions and being hearing-impaired doesn't mean you can't listen, just that you can't always hear'," she said, equally apologetic.

"So can we talk?" he asked.

She nodded. "I think we need to."

He dragged in a breath. "I had no idea Janine was going to turn up. I didn't even realize she still had a key to the apartment—and, just so we're clear, I changed all the furniture the month after she made it obvious she wasn't coming back. Including the bed."

"You didn't need to tell me that," she said, "but thank you." And it did feel better to know that the bed she'd shared with Tyler wasn't the bed he'd once shared with the love of his life.

He sighed. "I know you're not a gossip, and I'm not either—but I'm going to have to break Janine's confidence."

"You don't have to—" she began.

"Oh, but I do," he said, "because you need to know the full story about what she was doing here in the first place. When she left me, she took a job in Billings, running a big hotel. She ended up falling for the guy who owned the chain. And then she fell pregnant."

Remembering that Janine had lost the baby she'd made with Tyler, Stacey reached over to squeeze his hand. "It must have been hard for you to hear that."

"It was," he agreed, "but what made it worse was that the guy had lied to her about being separated from his wife. When she told him about the baby, he told her to get rid of it."

Stacey winced. "Did he know she'd lost your baby?"

"I have no idea—and I'm not sure it would've made a difference if he did," Tyler said.

"Poor Janine—that's horrible."

"So she walked out of her job," he said, "and went back to her mom in Bozeman. Except..." He grimaced. "Let's just say her mom had been in the same place as the other guy's wife, and Janine's news rubbed her up the wrong way. So Janine came here because she didn't know what else to do."

Alone and pregnant, rejected by her family… Stacey's heart went out to the other woman. "Poor Janine. I'm glad she had you to lean on." And she meant it.

"I wanted to tell you as soon as I realized that Janine had turned up here," he said, "so you wouldn't get the wrong idea and think that Janine and I… Well."

She bit her lip. "Sorry. I kind of jumped to conclusions."

"Janine said you'd called round. She didn't know about you and me at that point," he said, "so I'm guessing she might've given you the wrong impression."

"It might not've been deliberate. But she was only wearing your shirt, so I assumed…" Stacey grimaced. "I still should've talked to you about it. But you told me she was the love of your life, so I thought I was doing the right thing in stepping back. Letting you be with the woman you loved, instead of standing in your way."

"Janine was once the love of my life," he corrected, "but if I'm really honest with myself our relationship was heading for the rocks even before she lost the baby. When we broke up, it hurt. A lot. So it took me a long time to move on." He looked straight at her. "But I did move on. I met you."

"We haven't been together very long," she said.

"I know, but it's long enough for me to know."

"I thought you wanted Janine back."

He shook his head. "Even if I had, I would never have

just gone back to her without saying a word to you." He paused. "Is that what someone did to you in the past?"

She winced. "No, but if you want the truth I've been dumped the day after I took someone home to meet my parents. More than once. None of them could cope with my father."

Tyler smiled. "I'm not scared of your father."

"I'm not entirely sure he's going to like you," she admitted, "even if he ever does get back on speaking terms with me."

"Then we'll both have to put our egos aside and put you first," he said, "and that's exactly what I'll tell him."

"I'll have the emergency first aid kit on standby," she said dryly. "So what's happened to Janine? Where is she now?"

"I talked to her mom," Tyler said. "I made her realize that Janine really needed her—and also that Janine isn't the type to mess around with another woman's husband. And then Marie kind of calmed down and agreed to be there for her."

"But Janine didn't want to go to her mom's?"

"How did you guess?"

"I kind of eavesdropped," she admitted. "I was in my car the other morning when you both came into the parking lot."

He frowned. "So how is it possible to eavesdrop on a conversation outdoors, from the inside of a car on the other side of the parking lot?"

"I can lip-read," she said. "It wasn't something I consciously learned to do, but it got me through school before my hearing problem was diagnosed."

"So how much did you hear?" he asked.

"Just that she wanted to stay, but you said it had been over a long time ago." She paused. "And then you turned the corner so I couldn't see your faces anymore. End of conversation."

"What you missed," he said, "is me telling Janine that I'd found someone else. Someone I wanted to spend the rest of my life with. And I was sorry that she was going through such a tough time, but I wasn't the one for her."

Hope bloomed inside her. So was Tyler saying that *she* was the one he wanted?

He reached over to take her hand. "So I drove her back to Bozeman. She wasn't happy, and she mouthed off at her mom. There was a lot of talking, and I had to smooth ruffled feathers on both sides and make them talk to each other. It was so late by the time I thought it was safe me for me leave them on their own that her mom insisted I stay the night. And I knew it was way too late for me to call you and talk to you, so I stayed—and I bought apology flowers from the city before I came home."

"You didn't need the flowers," she said, "and you did try to talk to me. You sent me the text. It just never got to me."

"And because of that you ended up hurt," he said. "I feel bad about that."

"But it wasn't your fault. You're not the kind of man who goes round hurting people, and if I wasn't so du—"

"You are absolutely *not* dumb," he cut in. "But you've had your confidence cut from under you a few times. I can understand why you leapt to that conclusion."

"And Janine's beautiful."

"It's not all about the way someone looks," he said, "and I happen to think that a certain small, curvy special-needs teacher with unruly dark-blonde hair, grey-blue eyes, and a mouth that makes my pulse rate speed up is very beautiful indeed."

"I wasn't fishing for compliments."

"I know." He came round to her side of the table, scooped her up, sat down in her chair, and settled her on his lap. "Stacey Allman, I know it's been really fast, but I've fallen in love with you. It's everything about you. You're kind, you're honest, you're clever, and you make my world a better place."

She stared at him. He loved her? Really?

The question must've been written all over her face, because he said softly, "I love you. I think I have ever since the moment you rescued me from the smoke alarm—you didn't laugh at me, you didn't make me feel bad, and you just calmly sorted things out and showed me how to do it right. And then I noticed how cute you were. And the more time I spent talking to you, the more time I wanted to spend with you. It's everything about you."

She stroked his face. "I love you, too. I thought you were way out of my league."

He kissed her. "Never."

"You skate like an angel and I'm completely uncoordinated."

"You bake like an angel and I drop eggs," he countered. "It's fine. Between us we cover all the bases. We're two different halves of the same whole."

She thought about it. And she realized he was right. "The same whole."

He stole another kiss. "So. You and me. We're good?"

"We're good," she said. "Apart from one thing. It's the Bake-Off final tomorrow."

He sighed. "My cake is going to be completely terrible, because I haven't practiced baking—apart from that one cake we made last weekend."

"I thought Janine might help you."

"She doesn't cook, any more than I do," he said.

"We could do a practice run tonight," she said, "but you look all in."

"I am," he admitted, "and I can't do a practice tomorrow morning because I need to show my face at work. I've called in so many favors from my team this week, I'm really going to have to give them all a special bonus with their paycheck this month to say thanks and that I appreciate them having my back."

The fact he was thoughtful enough to recognize that he'd

expected a lot from his team meant that they wouldn't expect a bonus—they would've helped him anyway because they appreciated him, Stacey thought.

"The Bake-Off's all about raising money, not baking perfect cakes," she said.

"Yeah. I'll wing it," he said. "I have your recipe."

"I'll add some notes to remind you what to do if something goes skewy," she said. "And I'll make sure Jane McCullough puts that copy on your table."

"Thank you."

She kissed him. "You know what I think you need now?"

"What?"

"A bath," she said. "And an early night."

He smiled. "If that's an offer… Yes, please."

Chapter Thirteen

O N SATURDAY, TYLER brought Stacey a cup of coffee in bed. "With a spoonful of sugar," he said with a smile. "I'll see you at the Bake-Off."

"OK. Call me if you need anything," she said.

The final Bake-Off was being held at the Graff Hotel, in the glittery ballroom with its amazing chandeliers. The whole thing was starting with a luxurious formal cream tea, with biscuits and sandwiches; Stacey had bought her ticket early on, plus one for her aunt Joanie as a treat, and had arranged to meet Joanie there along with her friends from school and Tyler's gym.

Since its restoration, the Graff was even more splendid than it had been in its heyday; the grand lobby had rich paneled wood, marble floors and gleaming light fixtures. And the local media was out in full force, covering one of the glitziest events since the Valentine's Ball.

Stacey was chatting with her friends when Tara nudged her. "Your aunt Joanie's here."

Stacey looked round, ready to wave and smile—and

stopped dead in surprise.

Next to Joanie were the last two people she'd expected to see: Mary and Charles Allman.

Her parents.

"I... Excuse m-me a second," she said to Tara, and walked over to greet Joanie and her parents.

"Stacey. You look very nice," her father said, looking approvingly at the dress Stacey had bought for the occasion.

"Thank you. W-what are you doing here?" Stacey asked.

"Joanie met us from the train in Bozeman. She bought us a ticket to the event," Mary said.

Joanie added, "We've had a long overdue conversation and Charles has something to say to you—don't you, Charles?" She was smiling, but there was a definite hint of the strict schoolmistress Joanie had once been.

Charles looked at Stacey, took a deep breath, and announced, "I've thought about what you said and you were right."

Had she actually heard that right? Her father was admitting that he was wrong?

And then he shocked her even more by saying, "I'm sorry."

She'd never, ever heard her father apologize before. To anyone.

Joanie must really have taken him to task.

And it must've been difficult for him to force the words out. This was an olive branch she was going to grab with both hands. So she stepped forward and hugged him.

For a moment, Charles froze. And then he hugged her all the way back.

"For what it's worth," he said, "I *am* proud of you. I've never been good with children. The idea of doing what you do every day brings me out in hives—and even though I still think you'd have a better career in Missoula, if you want to be here then I guess I need to accept that and stop trying to manage your life."

Part of this felt like a parallel universe, where Stacey finally had the kind of parents she'd always wanted. "Thank you," she said, not quite believing that this was really happening.

"It's not going to be perfect between us," Charles warned. "I can't change who I am—but I'll try to be a better father to you."

"That's good enough for me. And I'll meet you halfway," Stacey said.

"Now that's settled," Joanie said, "I'm ready for my cream tea. Mary, shall we sit down? And Stacey can introduce us to all her friends."

IN ONE OF the smaller reception rooms, the bakers were gathered together and making sure that they all looked presentable for the photographer.

"I'm really dreading this," Tyler admitted. "I've baked this cake just once before."

"Man, even *I* practiced baking my cake more than once," Jake said. "You're taking one hell of a risk."

"I didn't have much choice. Let's just say it's been a week where I needed an extra twenty-four hours in every day," Tyler said dryly.

"I know how that feels," Matt said.

"Did your friend manage to touch base with my contact?" Warren asked.

"Yes—and I'm pleased to say she got the job," Tyler said.

"Good." Warren clapped his shoulder. "I'm glad it worked out."

"Me, too—and I owe you a lot of thanks for that," Tyler said.

"You'd do the same for any of us," Warren pointed out.

Jane came bustling in. "OK, bachelors, are you all ready to go? The photographer from the *Chronicle*'s here."

After they'd been photographed to within an inch of their lives, Jane led them out to the ballroom where everyone had been enjoying the special cream tea.

As before, tables were set up for each bachelor, with the ingredients, equipment and the recipe sheet for their particular dish, and a table for the judges. Zac Malone was the last to arrive, while the photographer was taking a last few shots of each bachelor.

Jodie Monroe introduced everyone for the last time and

thanked everyone for all the money they were raising toward Harry's House.

Tyler looked round the room for Stacey's table. He could see her aunt sitting next to her, and another older woman who looked enough like Joanie to be her sister, plus an old man. Then he did a double take. Had Stacey's parents actually turned up? He was prepared to drop everything he was doing and tell her father to back off if Stacey looked the slightest bit worried, but to his surprise she looked relaxed.

So had they made up their argument?

He hoped so, because he knew the row had hurt her deeply. But at the same time he also knew she'd needed to make a stand and let her father know that things between them had to change.

Jake nudged him. "Do you want to borrow some eggs now, or have you mastered juggling?"

Tyler laughed. "No, with this one you'd better hope I get the hand mixer on the right speed or you're going to be wearing sugar."

But to his relief he managed not to mess it up. As per Stacey's instructions, he kept the hand mixer on until the butter and sugar looked pale and fluffy; then he added the eggs without dropping them and got a whoop from the combined elementary school and Carter's Gym table, along with a thumbs-up from Jake.

He grated his fingers along with the orange rind, but he'd just have to live with that.

Carefully he folded in the flour and then added the milk, grateful that Stacey had added a handwritten note: *one tablespoon at a time, and check the dropping consistency from the spoon before you add more milk.*

As she'd promised, they let him use the ready-made liner rather than making him line the loaf tin with baking parchment. And then it was a matter of crossing his fingers, and putting his tin into the stove.

He juiced the orange and added the sugar, and waited to check that the cake was done. When he saw the middle had sunk and the edges looked a little bit too brown, he groaned inwardly. He was going to lose serious marks on presentation, but it was too late to do anything about that. He'd just have to hope that it tasted OK. He heated the juice and sugar mixture, spooned it carefully over the cake, and that was it. Just a matter of carrying the cake back to his table, setting it on the cooling rack, and hoping that the judges liked it.

After the judges had done their inspection and tasting and filled in the score sheets, Langdon Hale took the stage to announce the scores.

"In eighth place, with orange glaze cake, is Tyler Carter with a score of 35."

Given his total lack of practice, Tyler knew it was what he deserved. He'd let Stacey down.

"The scores from the three rounds have all been added together," Langdon said, "and I'm pleased to say that we have a definite winner—I'd like you all to congratulate Matt West."

The audience duly clapped and cheered.

"His prize is a free quarter-page ad in *The Courier* for ten weeks, his company name as a sponsor on the Chamber website for a year, his company name on the banner across Main Street for the Marietta Stroll and the Rodeo for one year, a sponsor brick outside Harry's House, and a room named for the company," Jane added.

"In second place is Wes St. Claire," Langdon said.

"And his prize is the company name on the website for the Chamber, the Rodeo banner, the Montana Stroll banner, and a sponsor brick outside Harry's House," Jane said.

"In a tie for third place we have Zac Malone and Warren Hunt," Langdon said.

"Third prize is the company name on the website for the Chamber, a choice of the name on either the Rodeo banner or the Montana Stroll banner, and a sponsor brick outside Harry's House," Jane said.

Langdon went though the list of bakers and, just as Tyler had suspected, he came last.

He said to Langdon, "As the loser, may I make a speech?"

The fire chief looked slightly surprised, but handed over the microphone.

"As the official worst Bachelor Baker," Tyler said, "I'd like to thank my fellow bakers for being good sports—and especially for lending me eggs when I dropped them."

The audience laughed, and he could see Stacey smiling.

"On their behalf I would also like to thank everyone who's supported us, from coaching us through to coming along to the event and buying raffle tickets."

There was a general murmur of approval.

"I'm glad to have been part of something so special and to help keep Harry Monroe's name alive. He was one of Marietta's best and I'm proud to have known him," Tyler continued. "One thing his death has taught me is that life is very short; and one thing the Bake-Off has taught me is that sometimes you need to take a risk. It doesn't matter that I came last in the competition, because over the course of the Bake-Off I won something really important—the heart of the sweetest woman I've ever met. So, Stacey Allman…" He dropped to one knee. "Would you do me the honor of being my wife?"

Charles Allman stood up and cleared his throat. "Aren't you supposed to ask my permission before you propose to my daughter?"

"No," Tyler said, still on one knee, "because this is the twenty-first century and women aren't possessions—they make their own choices. Your daughter is an amazing woman and I love her very much, and I very much hope that I can welcome you to my family."

"Then in that case," Charles said, "I should let Stacey speak for herself."

"Will you marry me, Stacey?" Tyler asked softly.

Please let her say yes, he begged inwardly.

Please let me not have rushed her into this.

Please let this go right.

She took a deep breath. "Y-yes."

The rest of whatever she said was lost in a roar of approval and cheering.

Jane grabbed the microphone. "Well, I wasn't expecting this as part of the Bake-Off, but I'm very pleased for all of you. Congratulations."

"It's not every day your only daughter gets engaged," Charles said. "Welcome to the family, Tyler. And I'd like to buy everyone here a glass of champagne or whatever they'd like to drink, to toast my daughter and my new son-in-law-to-be."

The waiters came up to take drink orders while Jane auctioned off the remaining cake. Tyler, sitting at the elementary school and Carter's Gym table with Stacey and her family, made sure he put in a winning bid for his orange glazed cake.

"You don't have any faith in your baking ability, Tyler?" Charles asked.

"I can do a lot of things," Tyler said, "but baking isn't my forte—even with help from Stacey."

"It takes guts to get up and do that kind of thing in public, especially when you know you're going to do badly," Charles mused.

"I wasn't the only one, and it's for a good cause," Tyler said.

"Stacey was telling me about it." Charles looked thoughtful. "Excuse me a moment, would you?"

When he came back, Stacey asked, "Was there a problem?"

"No. I just wanted to make a semi-anonymous donation," Charles said. "I had a word with the organizer to sort out the details of where to send the money."

Stacey stared at her father in surprise. This wasn't the way her father did things. He always made sure he got public acknowledgement about everything he did. Or maybe this was proof that he was trying to change.

"We're staying at the Graff for a couple of days," Mary said. "Maybe we can all have dinner here tonight so we can get to know Tyler better. And maybe you can both show us around the town."

"I'd like that," Tyler said. "Stacey?"

She nodded. "It works for me."

"Good. Here's to new beginnings." He lifted his glass, and they drank a toast. "And especially here's to Stacey," he said, "and her spoonful of sugar."

The End

You'll love the next book in the…

Bachelor Bake-Off series

Book 1: *A Teaspoon of Trouble* by Shirley Jump

Book 2: *A Spoonful of Sugar* by Kate Hardy

Book 3: *Sprinkled with Love* by Jennifer Faye

Book 4: *Baking for Keeps* by Jessica Gilmore

Book 5: *A Recipe for Romance* by Lara Van Hulzen

Available now at your favorite online retailer!

About the Author

Kate Hardy is the award-winning author of more than 60 novels for Harlequin, Entangled and Tule Publishing.

She lives in Norwich in the east of England with her husband, two teenage children, a springer spaniel called Byron, and too many books to count. She's a bit of a science and history nerd who loves cinema, the theatre, and baking (which is why you'll find her in the gym five mornings a week – oh, and to ballroom dancing lessons). She loves doing research, especially if it means something hands-on and exploring. (That's how the ballroom dancing started…)

Thank you for reading

A Spoonful of Sugar

If you enjoyed this book, you can find more from all our great authors at TulePublishing.com, or from your favorite online retailer.

TULE
PUBLISHING

CPSIA information can be obtained
at www.ICGtesting.com
Printed in the USA
LVHW090956090419
613492LV00001B/31/P

9 781946 772091